A Buzz Beaker Brainstorm

WIND POWER WHIZ KID

Librarian Reviewer
Katharine Kan
Graphic novel reviewer and Library Consultant, Panama City, FL
MLS in Library and Information Studies, University of Hawaii at
Manoa, HI

Reading Consultant
Elizabeth Stedem
Educator/Consultant, Colorado Springs, CO
MA in Elementary Education, University of Denver, CO

STONE ARCH BOOKS
www.stonearchbooks.com

Graphic Sparks are published by Stone Arch Books
151 Good Counsel Drive, P.O. Box 669
Mankato, Minnesota 56002
www.stonearchbooks.com

Library of Congress Cataloging-in-Publication Data
Nickel, Scott.
Wind Power Whiz Kid: A Buzz Beaker Brainstorm / by Scott Nickel; illustrated by Andy J. Smith.
p. cm. — (Graphic Sparks. Buzz Beaker)
ISBN 978-1-4342-0758-6 (library binding)
ISBN 978-1-4342-0854-5 (pbk.)
1. Graphic novels. [1. Graphic novels. 2. Inventors—Fiction. 3. Inventions—Fiction.] I. Smith, Andy J., 1975– ill. II. Title.
PZ7.7.N53Wi 2009
[Fic]—dc22 2008006713

Summary: Buzz Beaker's dad invents an eco-friendly windmill to power the entire town. Unfortunately, the not-so-friendly Mr. Sludgeco wants it destroyed before his planet-polluting power plant goes out of business. Can brainy Buzz and his friends stop Sludgeco's explosive plans?

Art Director: Heather Kindseth
Graphic Designer: Brann Garvey

1 2 3 4 5 6 13 12 11 10 09 08

9999Printed in the United States of America

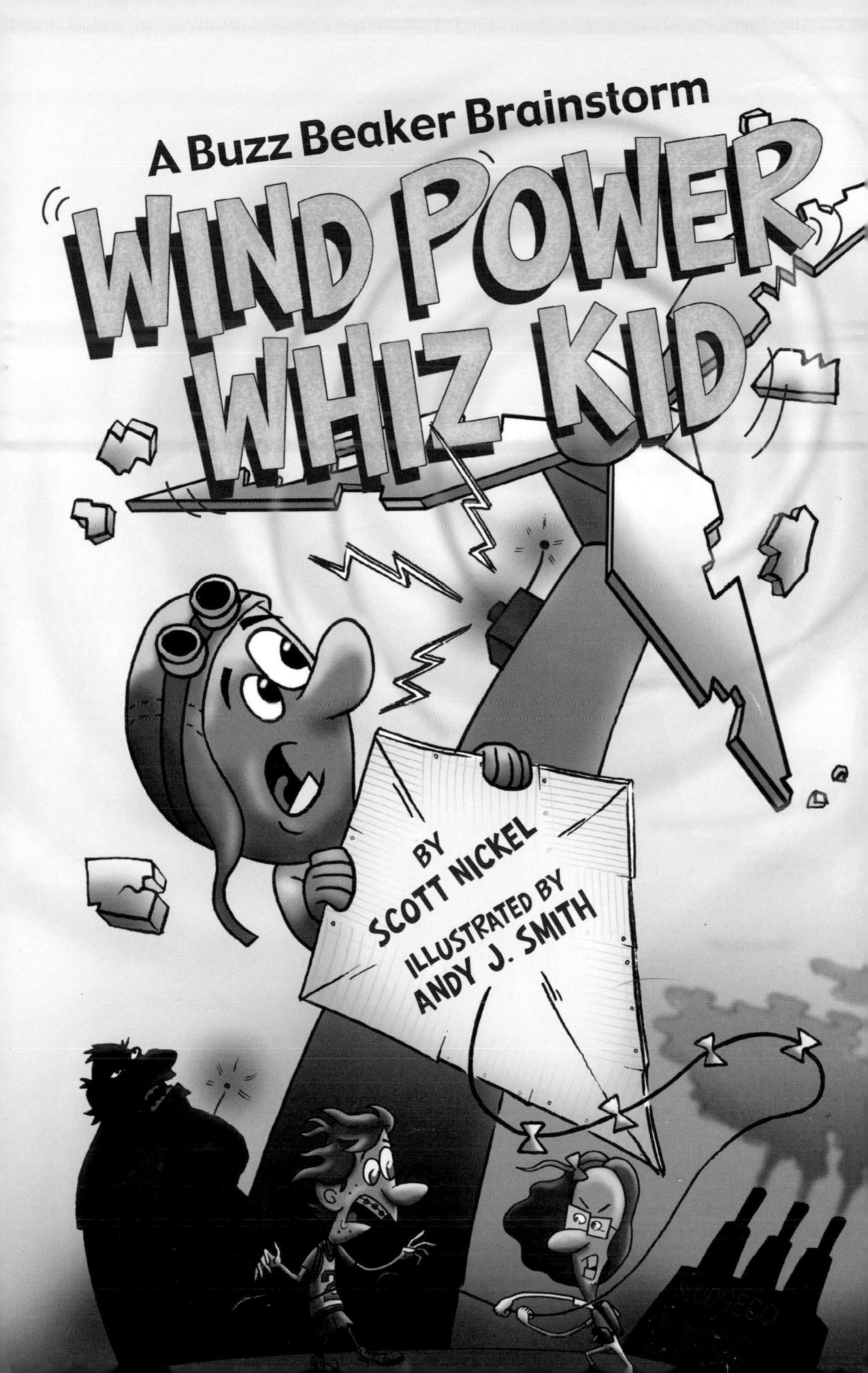
A Buzz Beaker Brainstorm
WIND POWER WHIZ KID
BY
SCOTT NICKEL
ILLUSTRATED BY
ANDY J. SMITH

CAST OF CHARACTERS

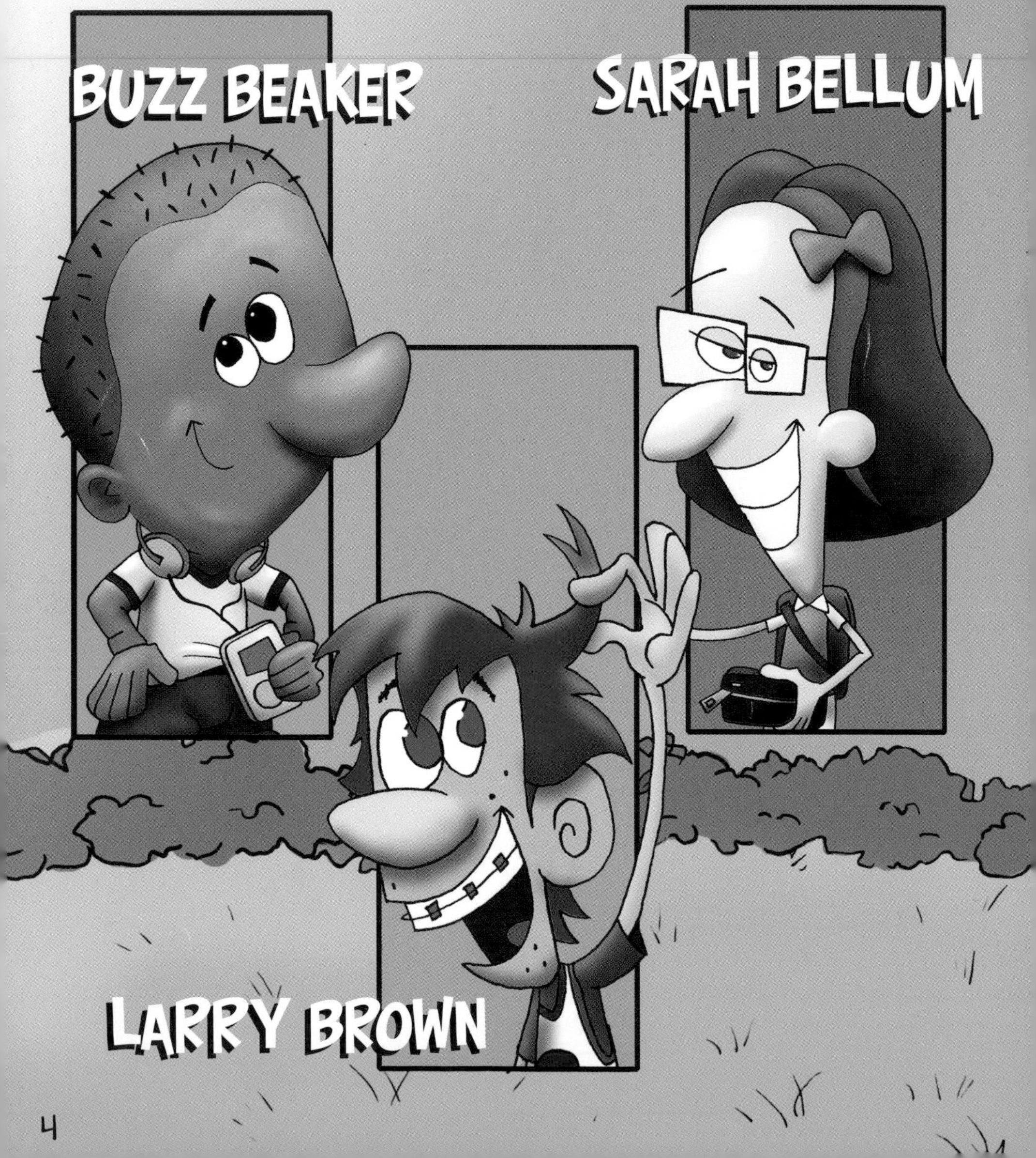
BUZZ BEAKER
SARAH BELLUM
LARRY BROWN

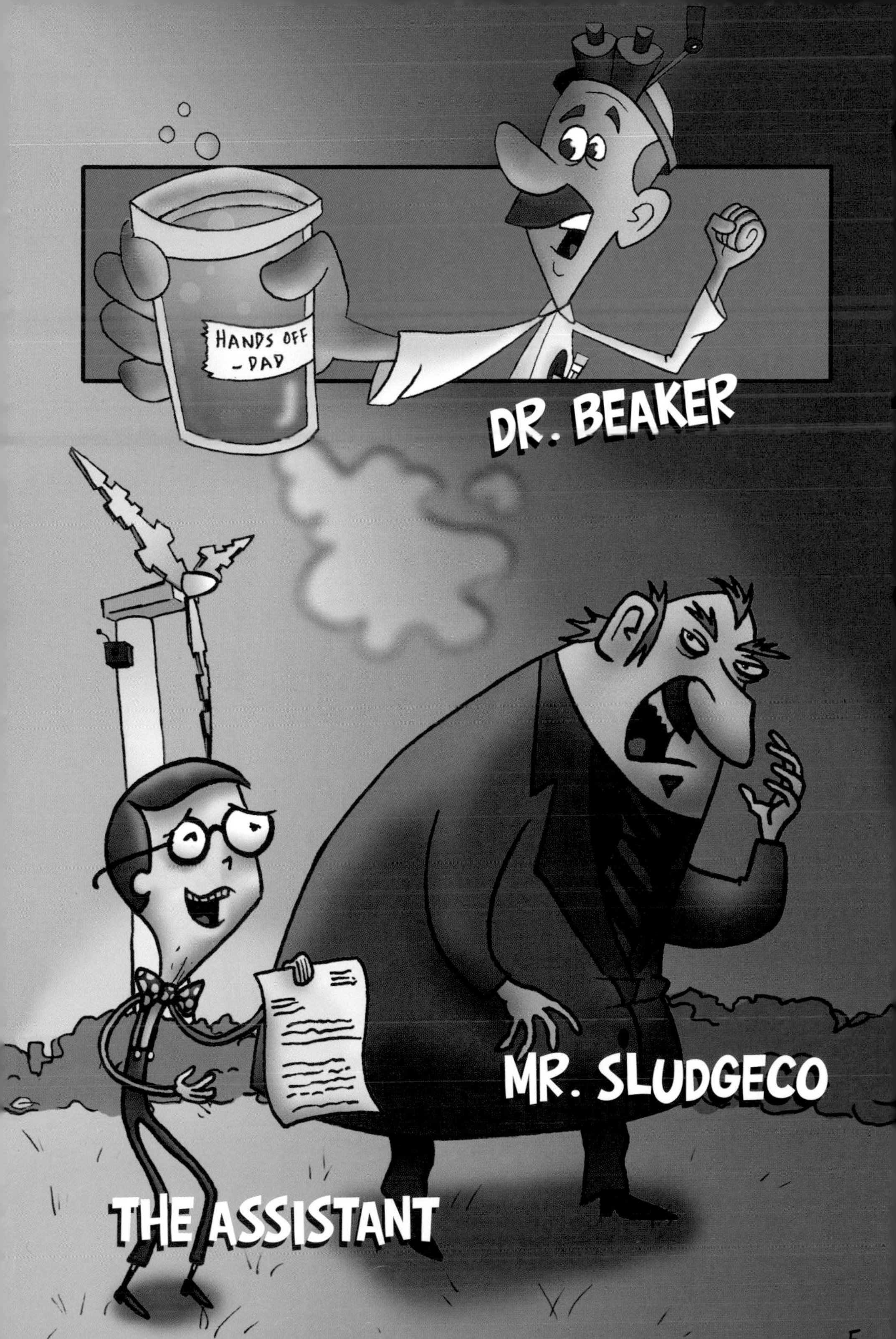
HANDS OFF
-DAD
DR. BEAKER
MR. SLUDGECO
THE ASSISTANT

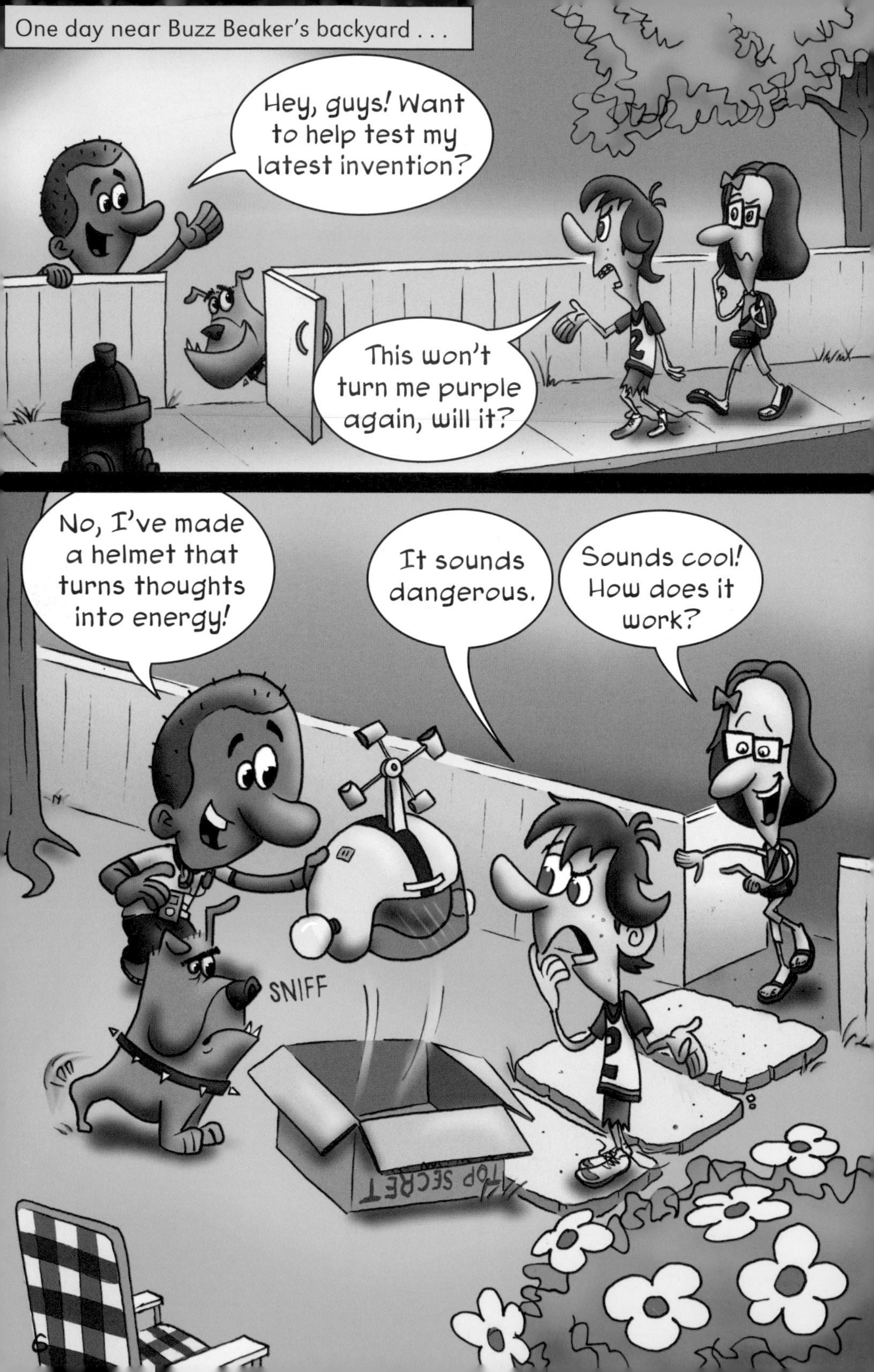
One day near Buzz Beaker's backyard . . .
Hey, guys! Want to help test my latest invention?
This won't turn me purple again, will it?
No, I've made a helmet that turns thoughts into energy!
It sounds dangerous.
Sounds cool! How does it work?
SNIFF
TOP SECRET

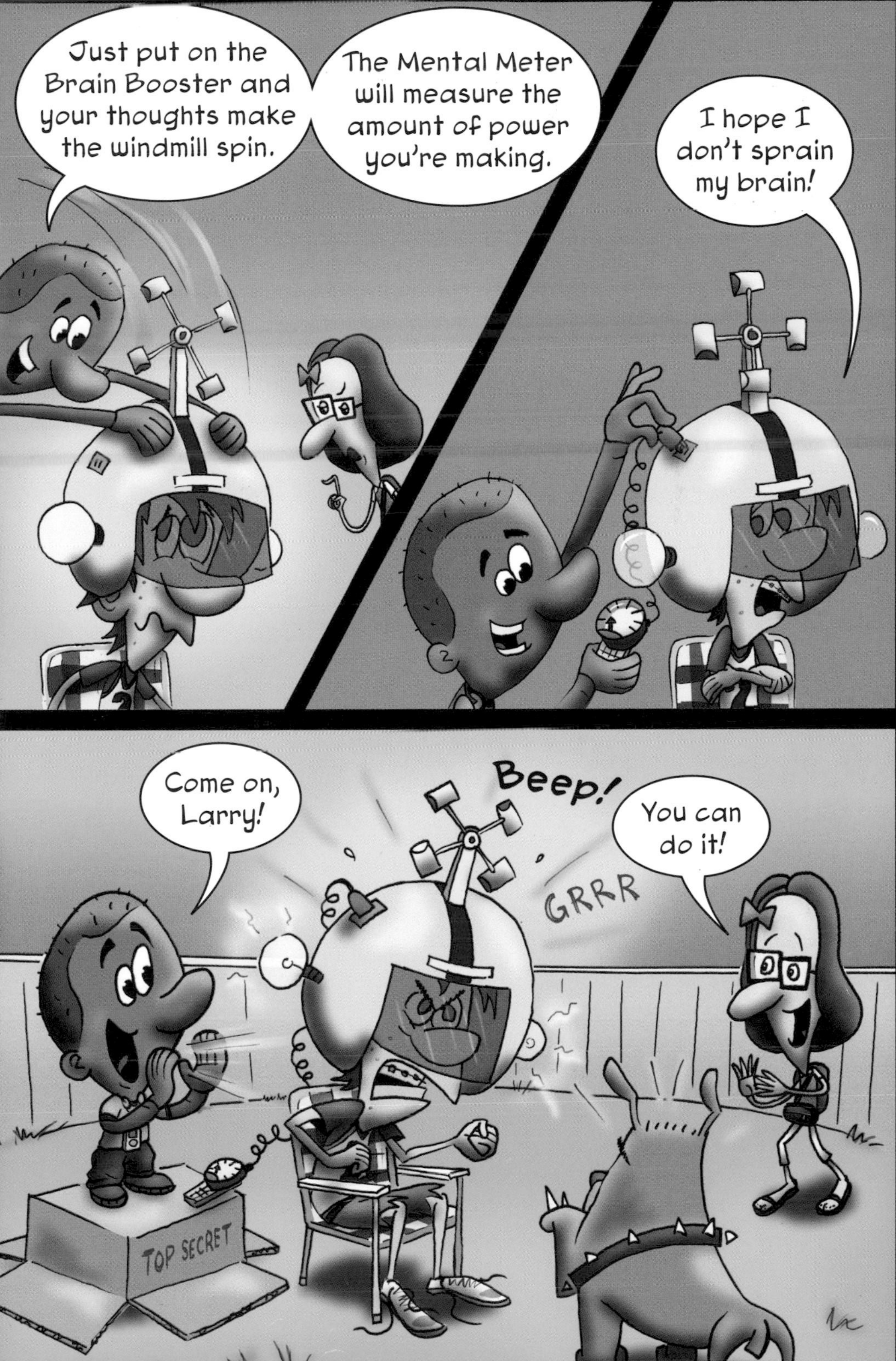
Just put on the Brain Booster and your thoughts make the windmill spin.
The Mental Meter will measure the amount of power you're making.
I hope I don't sprain my brain!
Come on, Larry!
Beep!
GRRR
You can do it!
TOP SECRET

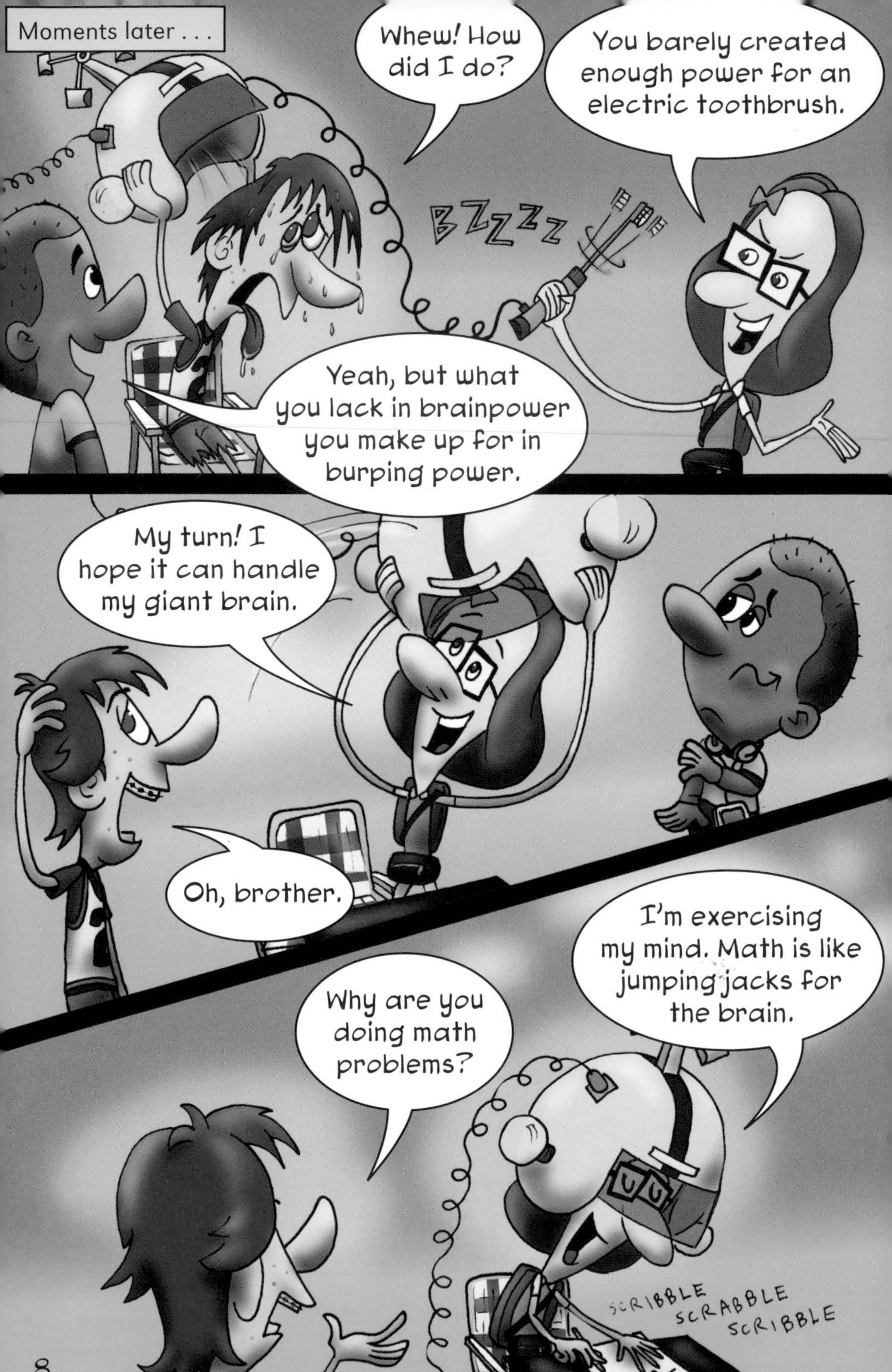
Moments later . . .
Whew! How did I do?
You barely created enough power for an electric toothbrush.
BZZZZZ
Yeah, but what you lack in brainpower you make up for in burping power.
My turn! I hope it can handle my giant brain.
Oh, brother.
Why are you doing math problems?
I'm exercising my mind. Math is like jumping jacks for the brain.
SCRIBBLE SCRABBLE SCRIBBLE

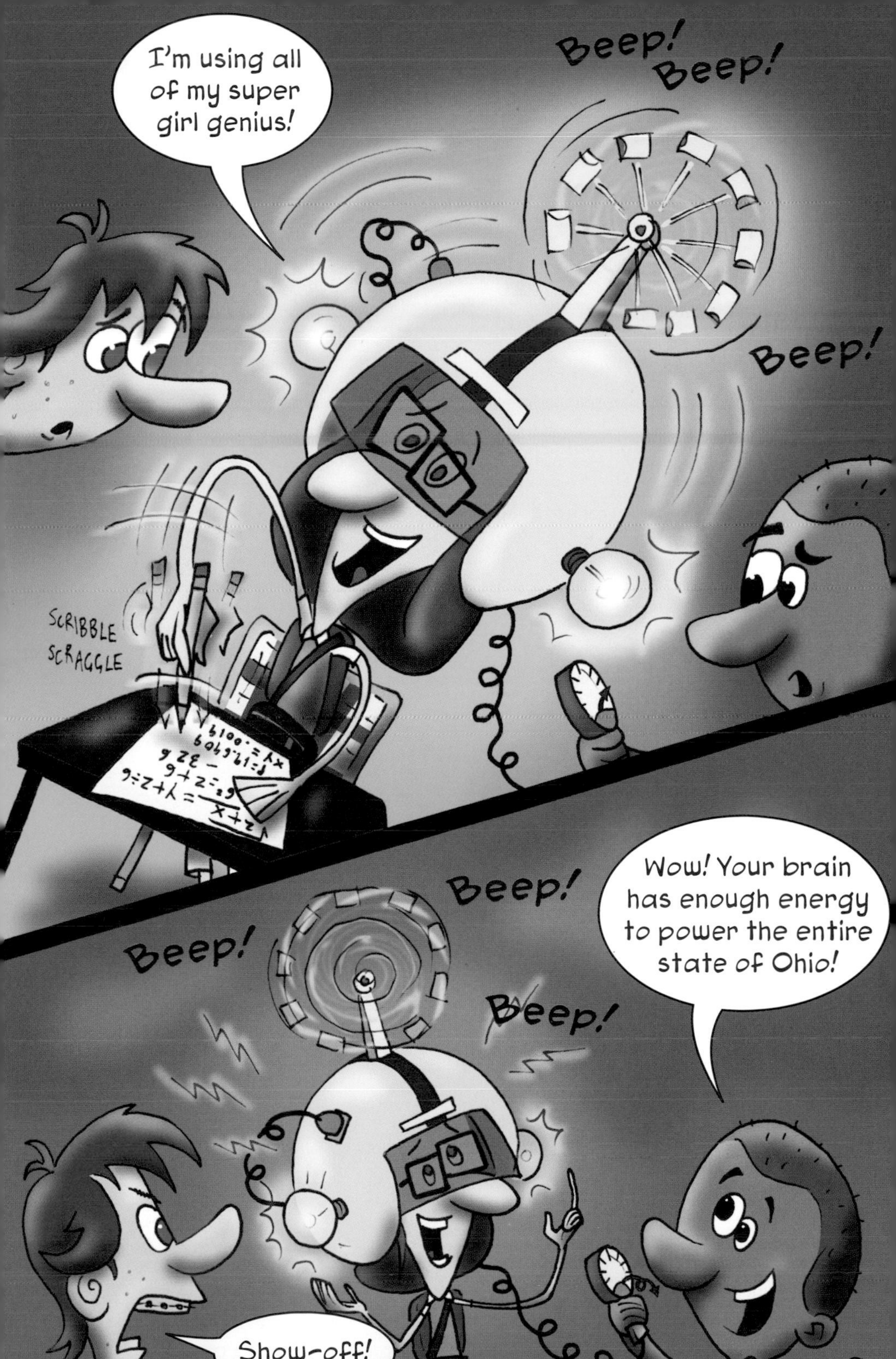
I'm using all of my super girl genius!
Beep! Beep!
Beep!
SCRIBBLE SCRAGGLE
Beep!
Beep!
Beep!
Wow! Your brain has enough energy to power the entire state of Ohio!
Show-off!

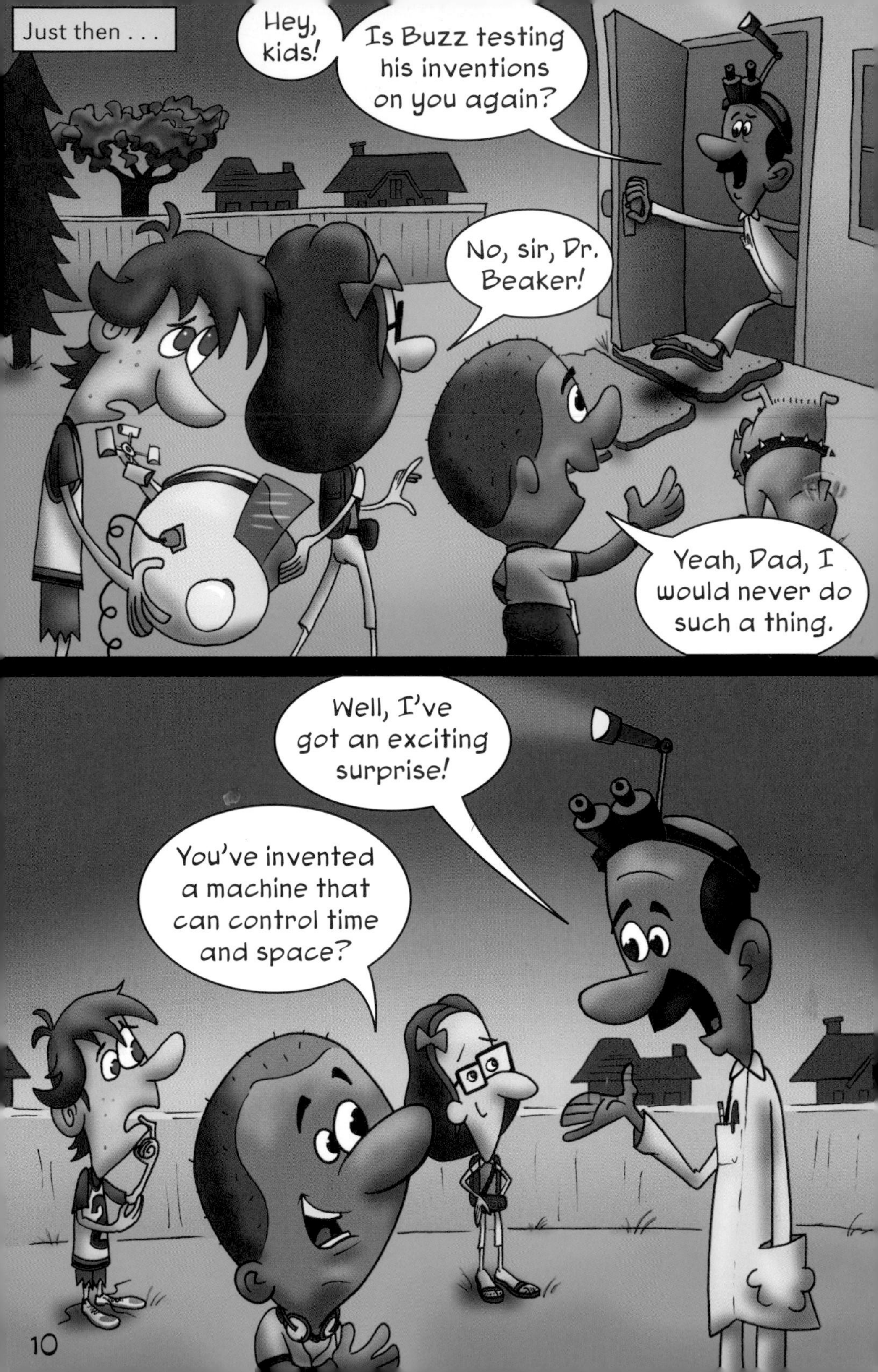
Just then . . .
Hey, kids!
Is Buzz testing his inventions on you again?
No, sir, Dr. Beaker!
Yeah, Dad, I would never do such a thing.
Well, I've got an exciting surprise!
You've invented a machine that can control time and space?

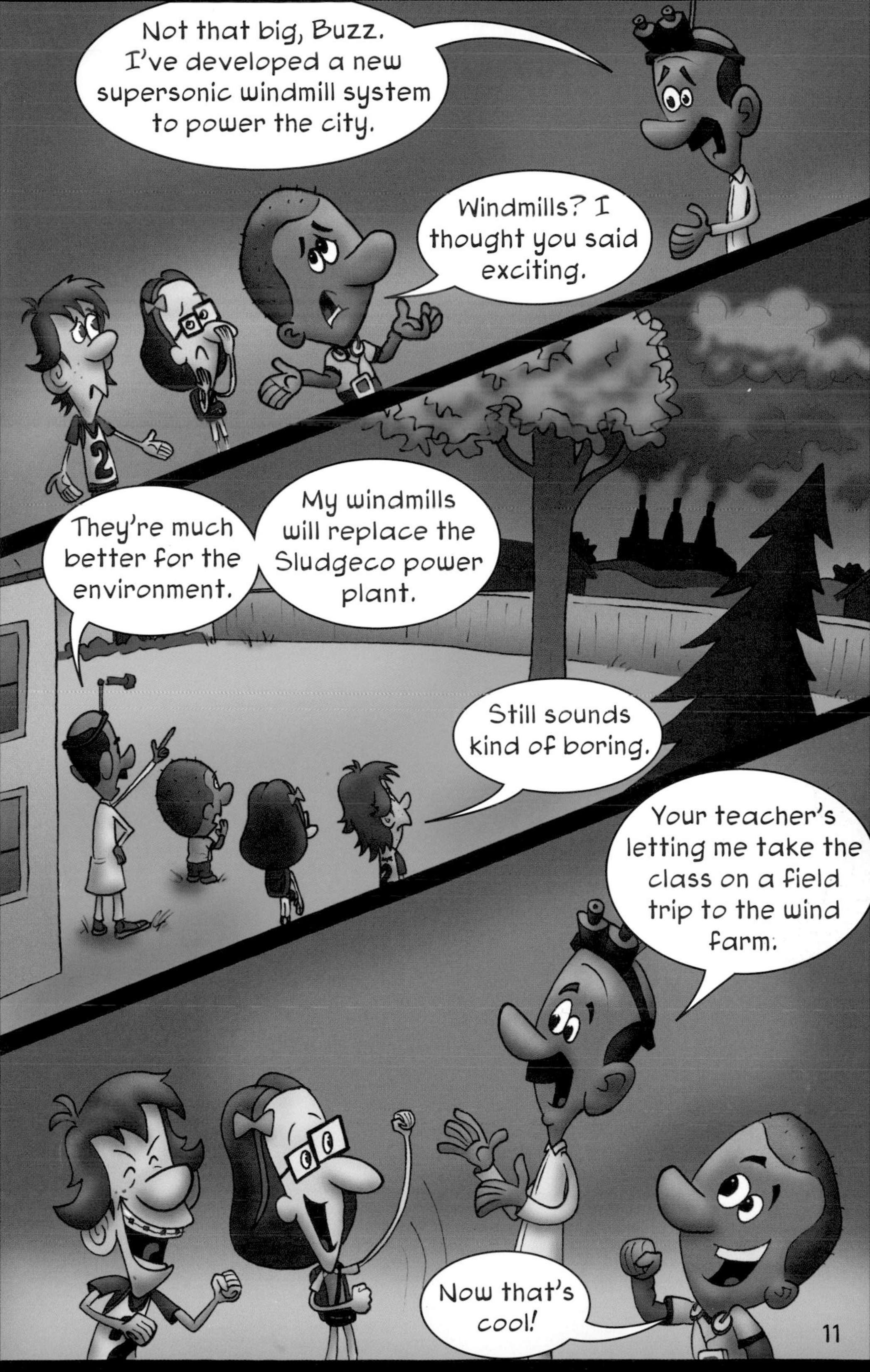
Not that big, Buzz. I've developed a new supersonic windmill system to power the city.
Windmills? I thought you said exciting.
They're much better for the environment.
My windmills will replace the Sludgeco power plant.
Still sounds kind of boring.
Your teacher's letting me take the class on a field trip to the wind farm.
Now that's cool!

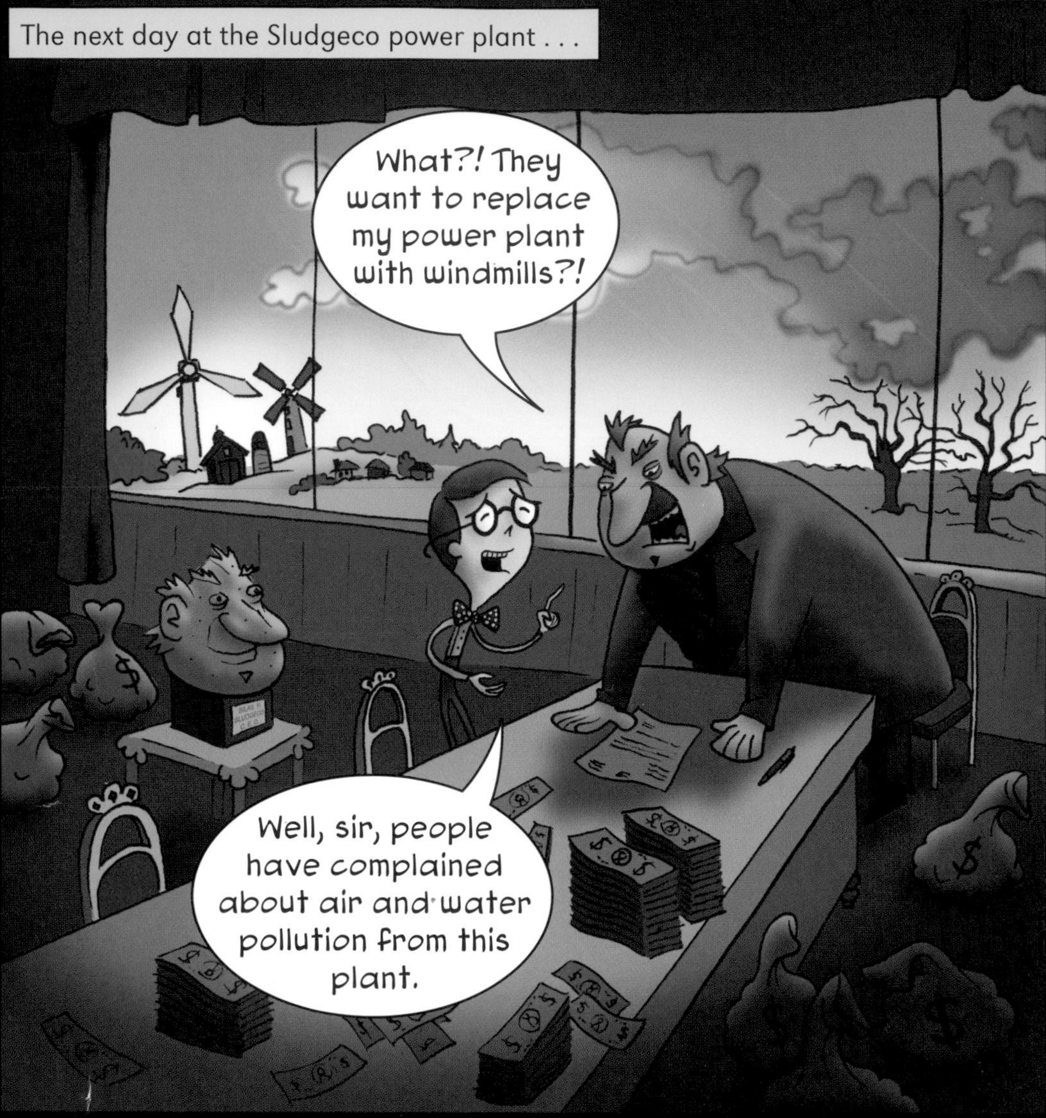
The next day at the Sludgeco power plant . . .
What?! They want to replace my power plant with windmills?!
Well, sir, people have complained about air and water pollution from this plant.

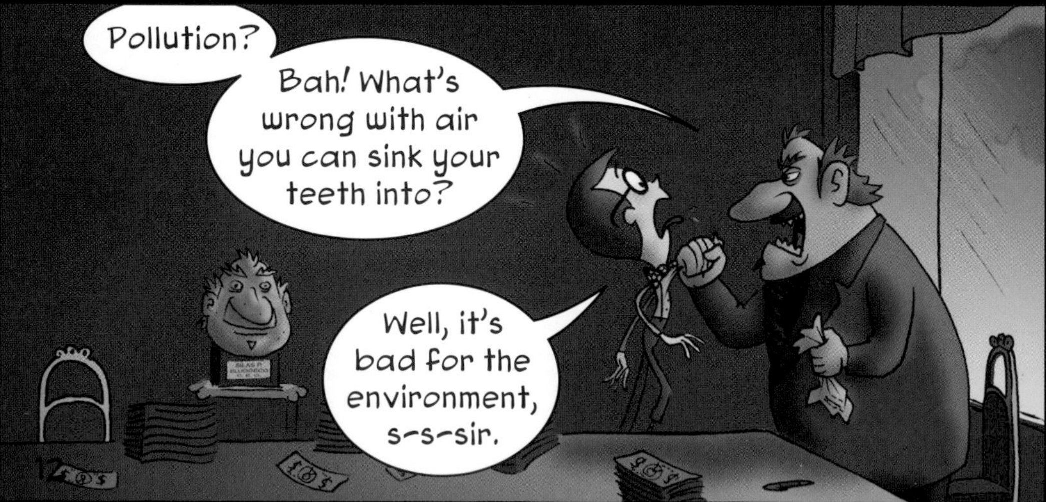
Pollution?
Bah! What's wrong with air you can sink your teeth into?
Well, it's bad for the environment, s-s-sir.

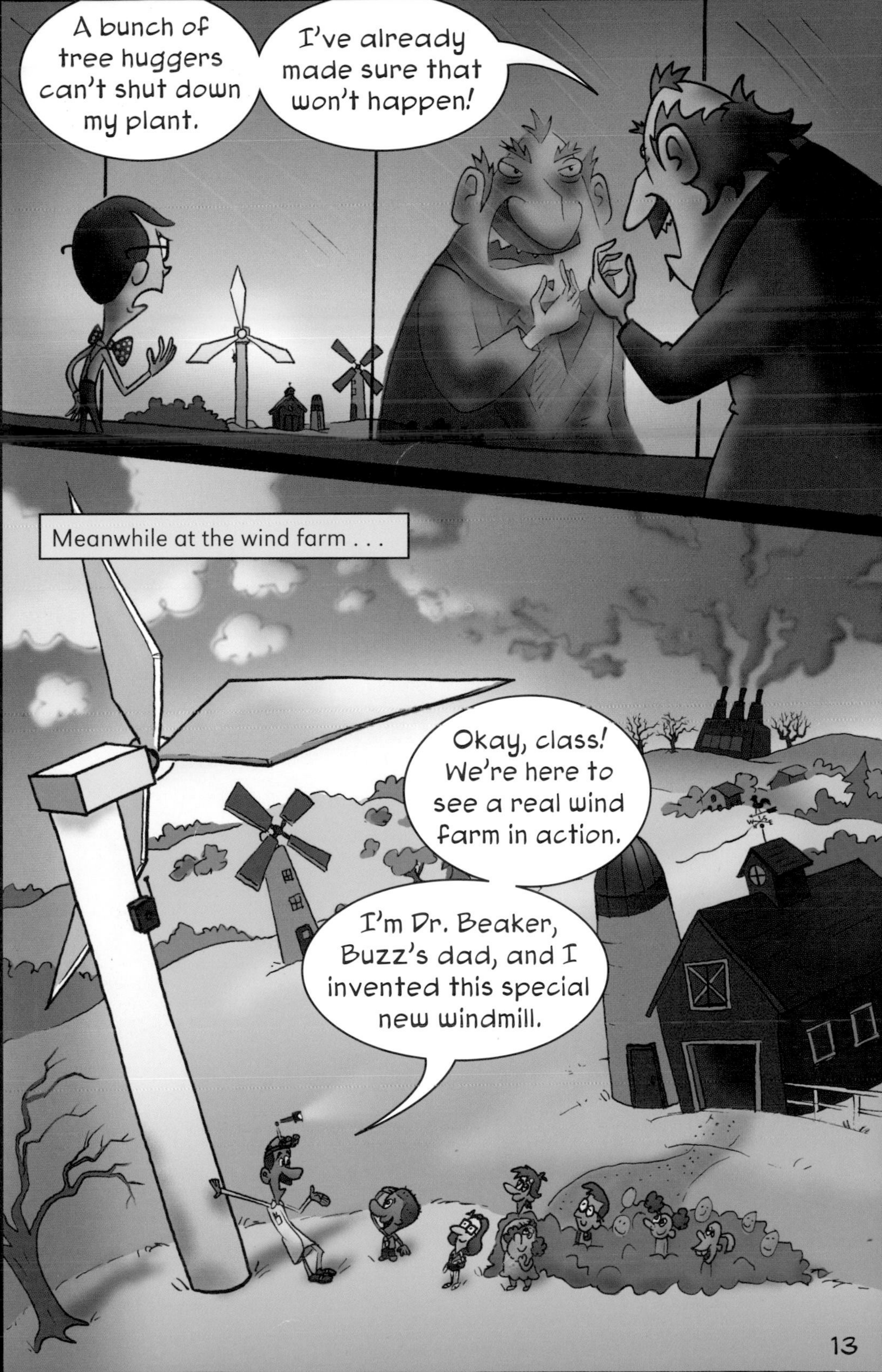
A bunch of tree huggers can't shut down my plant.
I've already made sure that won't happen!
Meanwhile at the wind farm . . .
Okay, class! We're here to see a real wind farm in action.
I'm Dr. Beaker, Buzz's dad, and I invented this special new windmill.

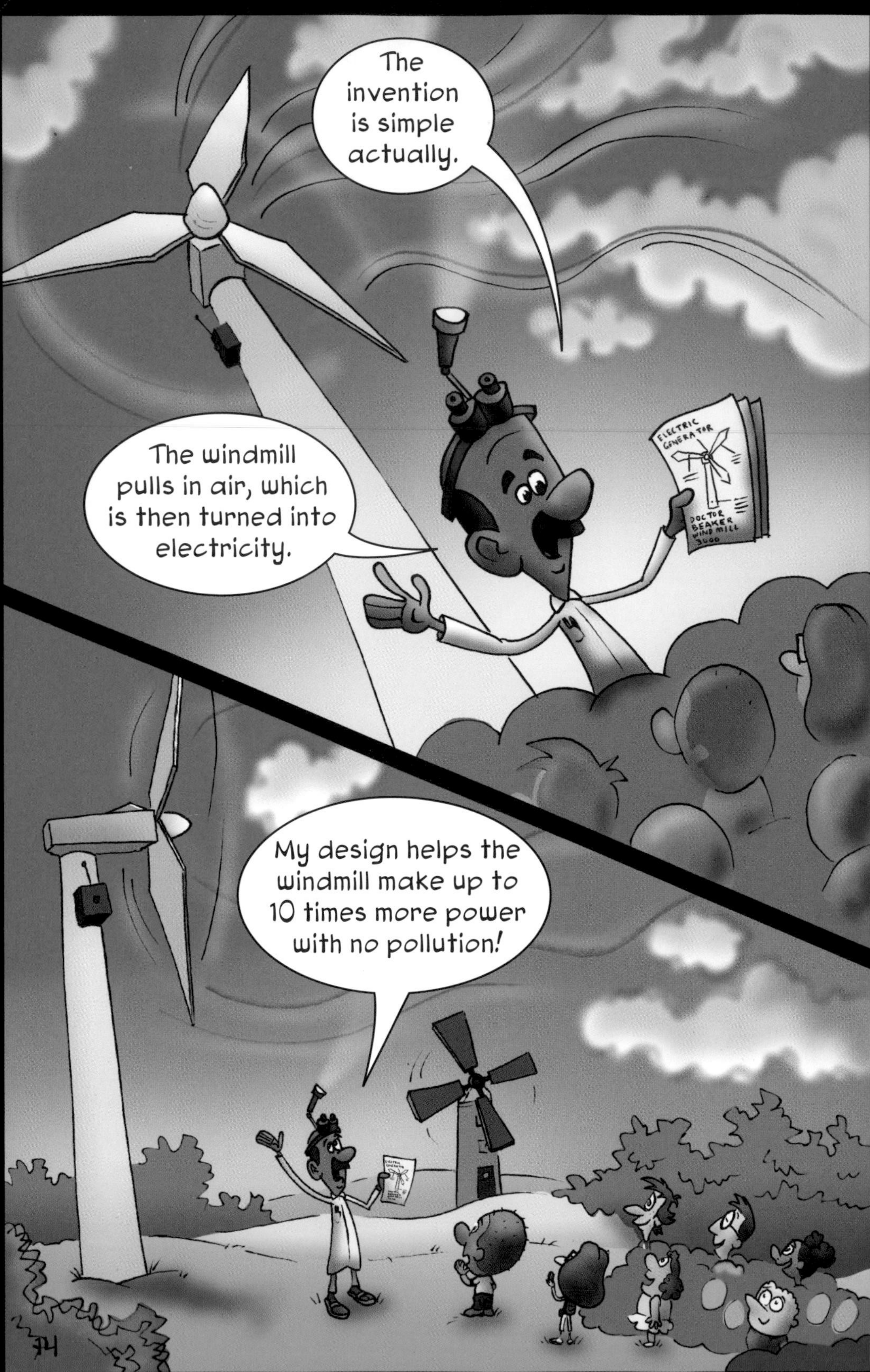
The invention is simple actually.
ELECTRIC GENERATOR
DOCTOR BEAKER WIND MILL 3000
The windmill pulls in air, which is then turned into electricity.
My design helps the windmill make up to 10 times more power with no pollution!

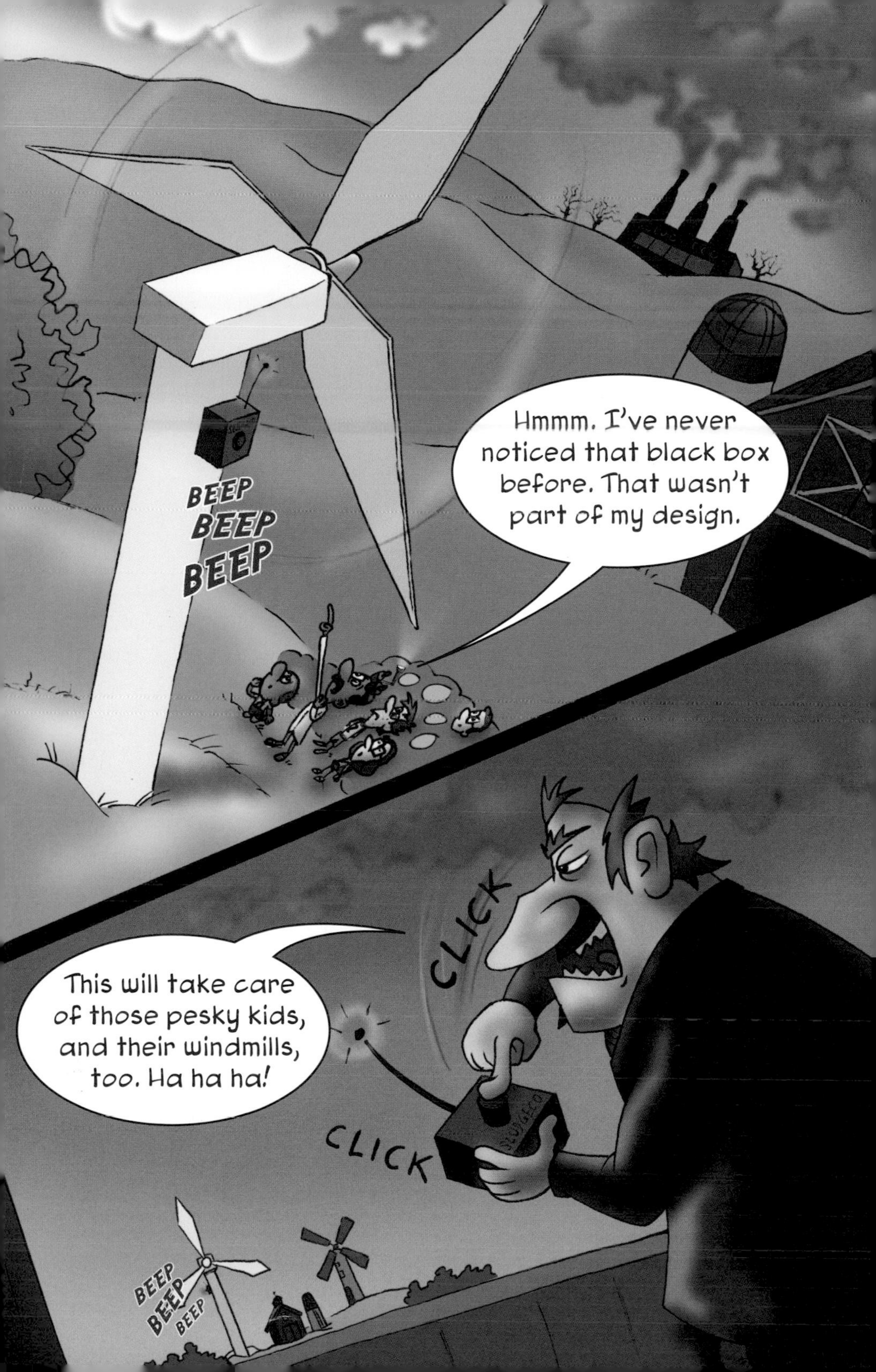
BEEP
BEEP
BEEP
Hmmm. I've never noticed that black box before. That wasn't part of my design.
CLICK
This will take care of those pesky kids, and their windmills, too. Ha ha ha!
CLICK
BEEP
BEEP
BEEP

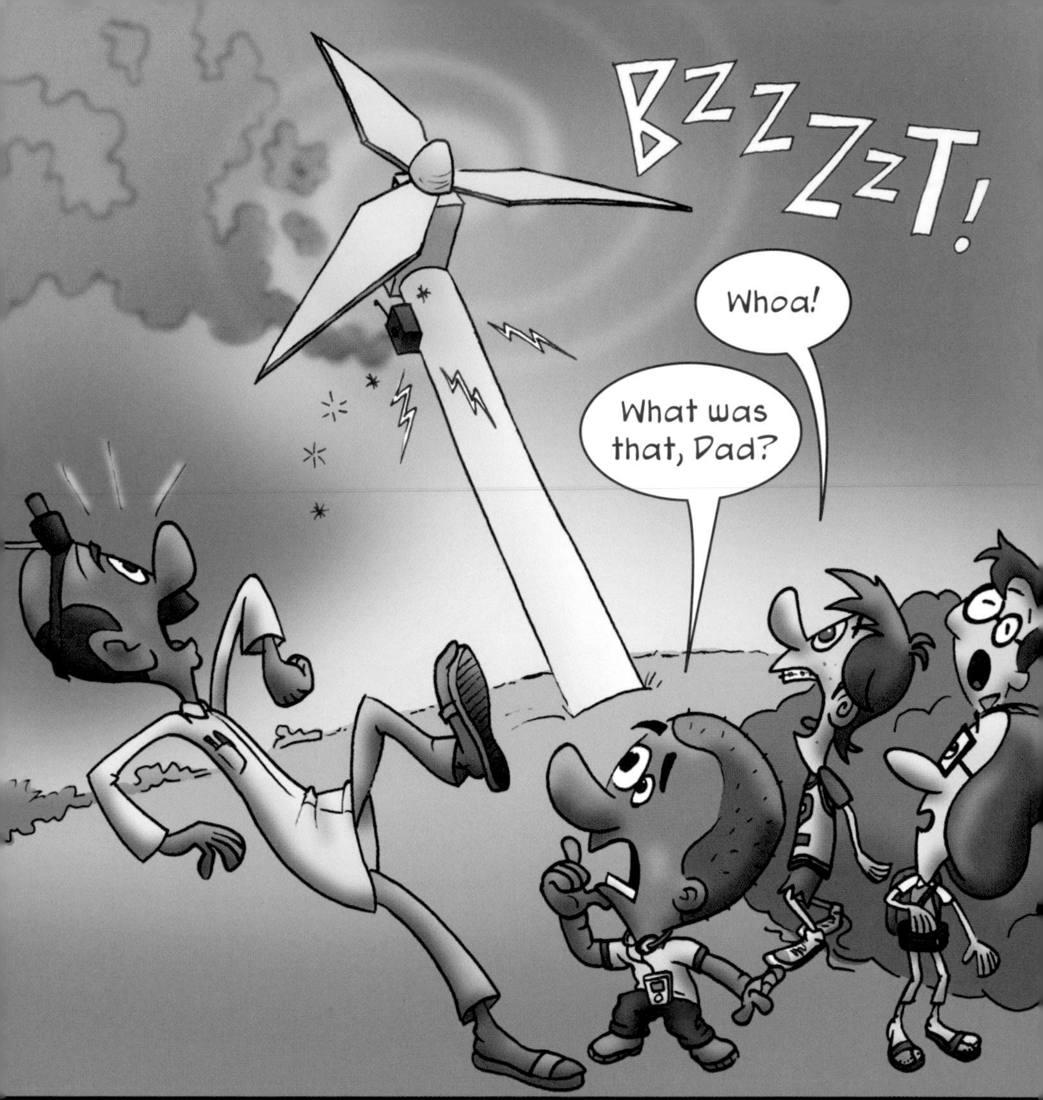
BZZZZZT!
Whoa!
What was that, Dad?

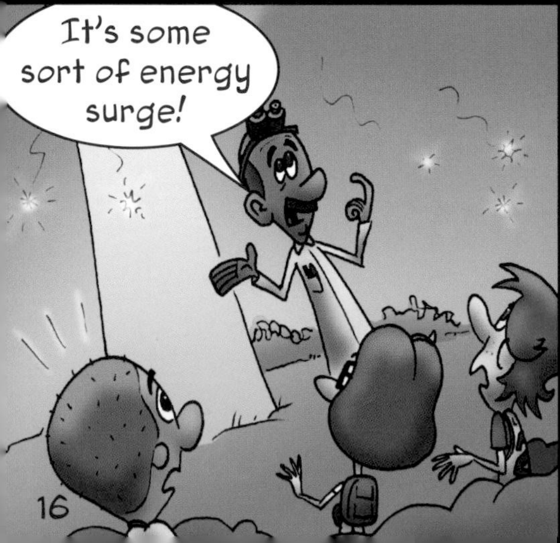
It's some sort of energy surge!

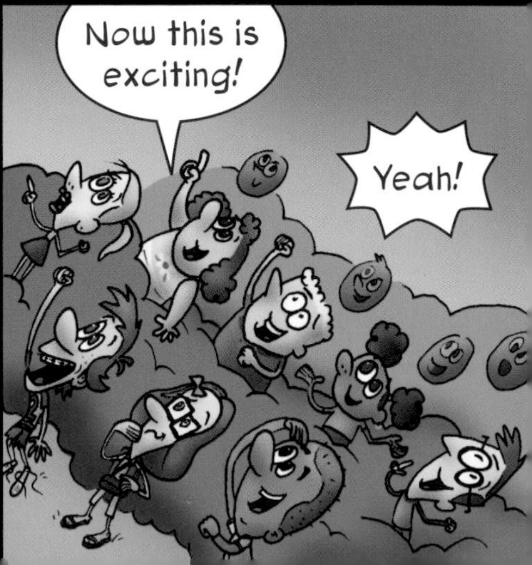
Now this is exciting!
Yeah!

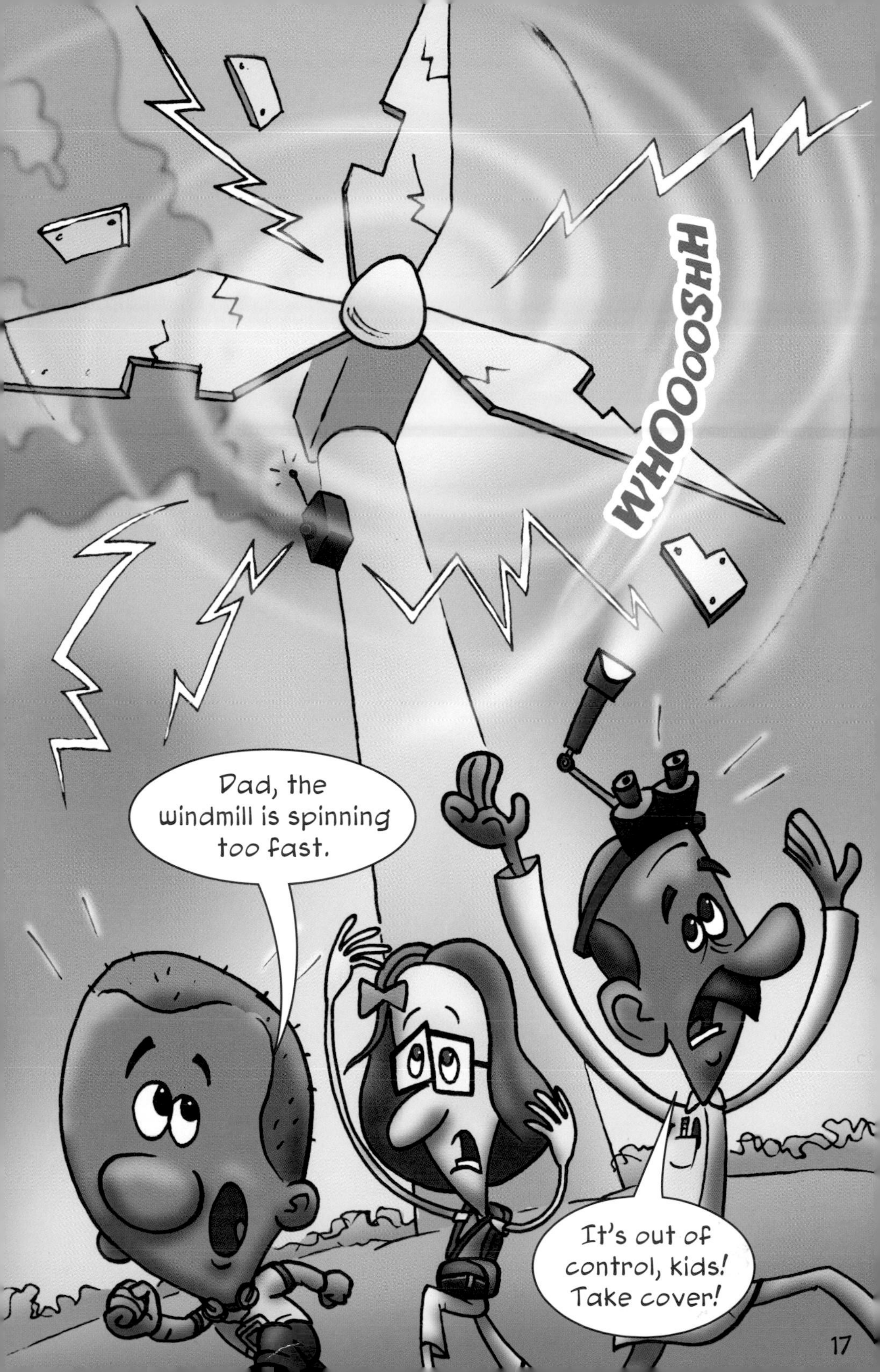
WHOOOOSHH
Dad, the windmill is spinning too fast.
It's out of control, kids! Take cover!

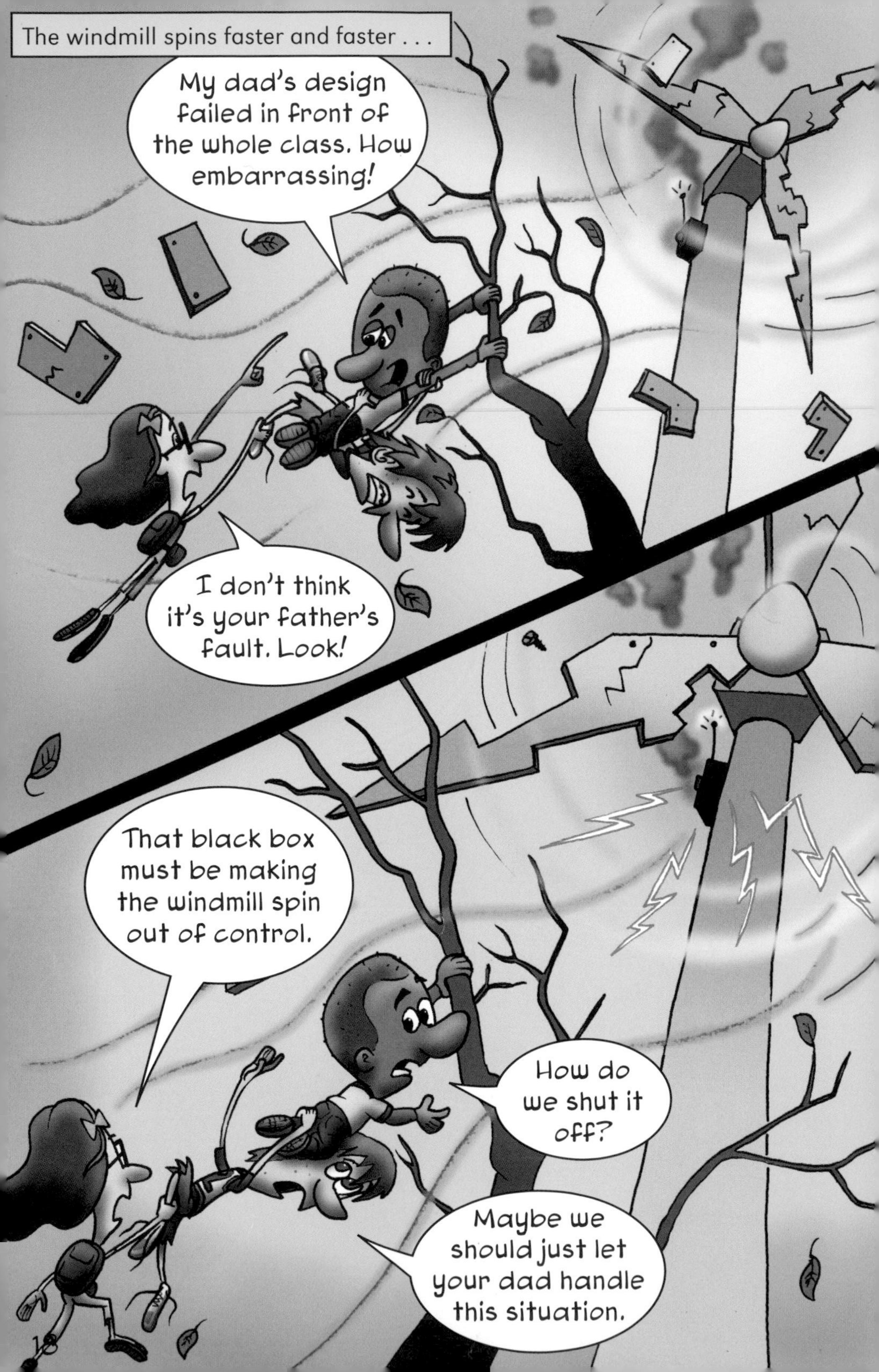
The windmill spins faster and faster . . .
My dad's design failed in front of the whole class. How embarrassing!
I don't think it's your father's fault. Look!
That black box must be making the windmill spin out of control.
How do we shut it off?
Maybe we should just let your dad handle this situation.

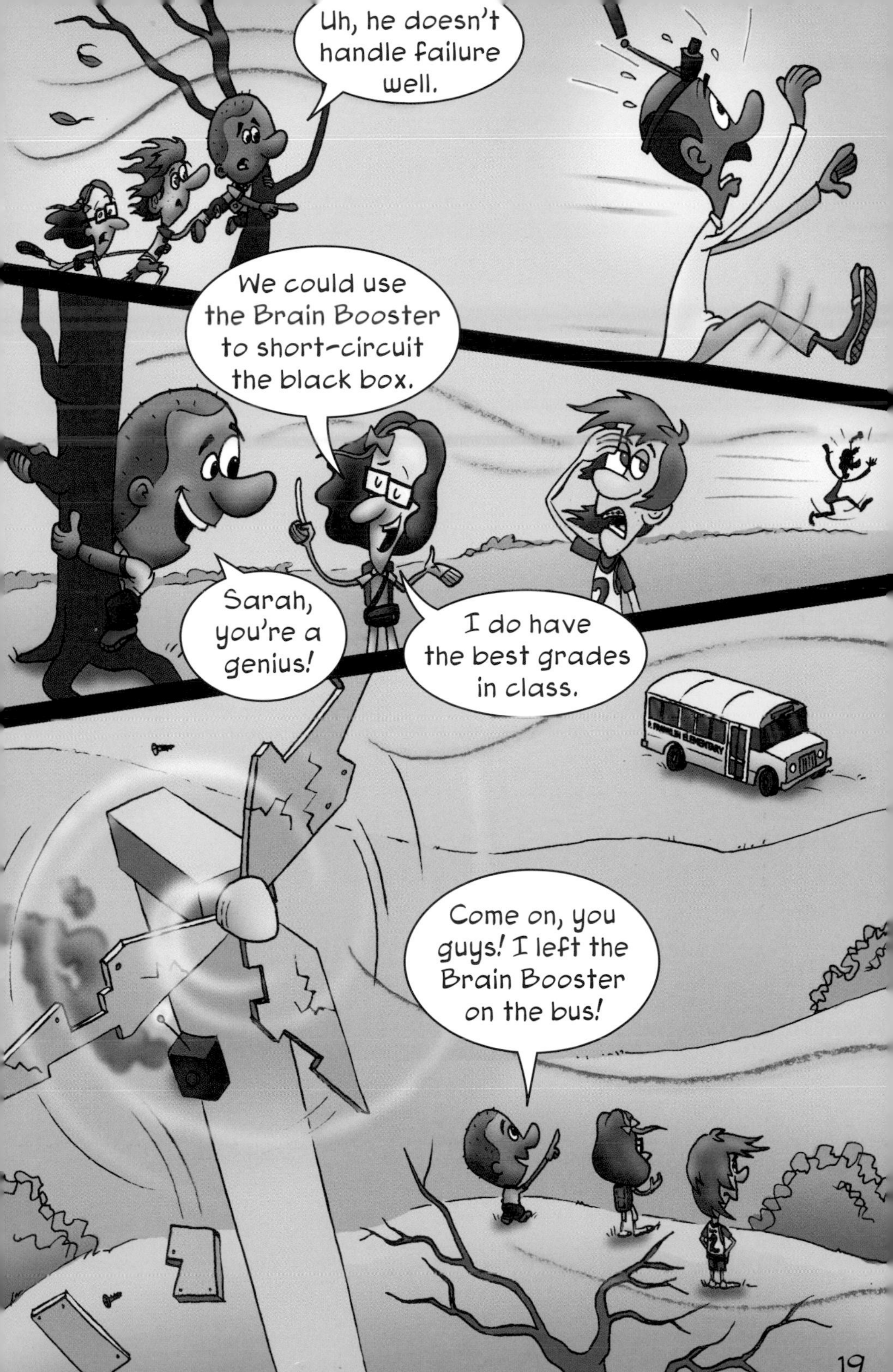

Uh, he doesn't handle failure well.
We could use the Brain Booster to short-circuit the black box.
Sarah, you're a genius!
I do have the best grades in class.
Come on, you guys! I left the Brain Booster on the bus!

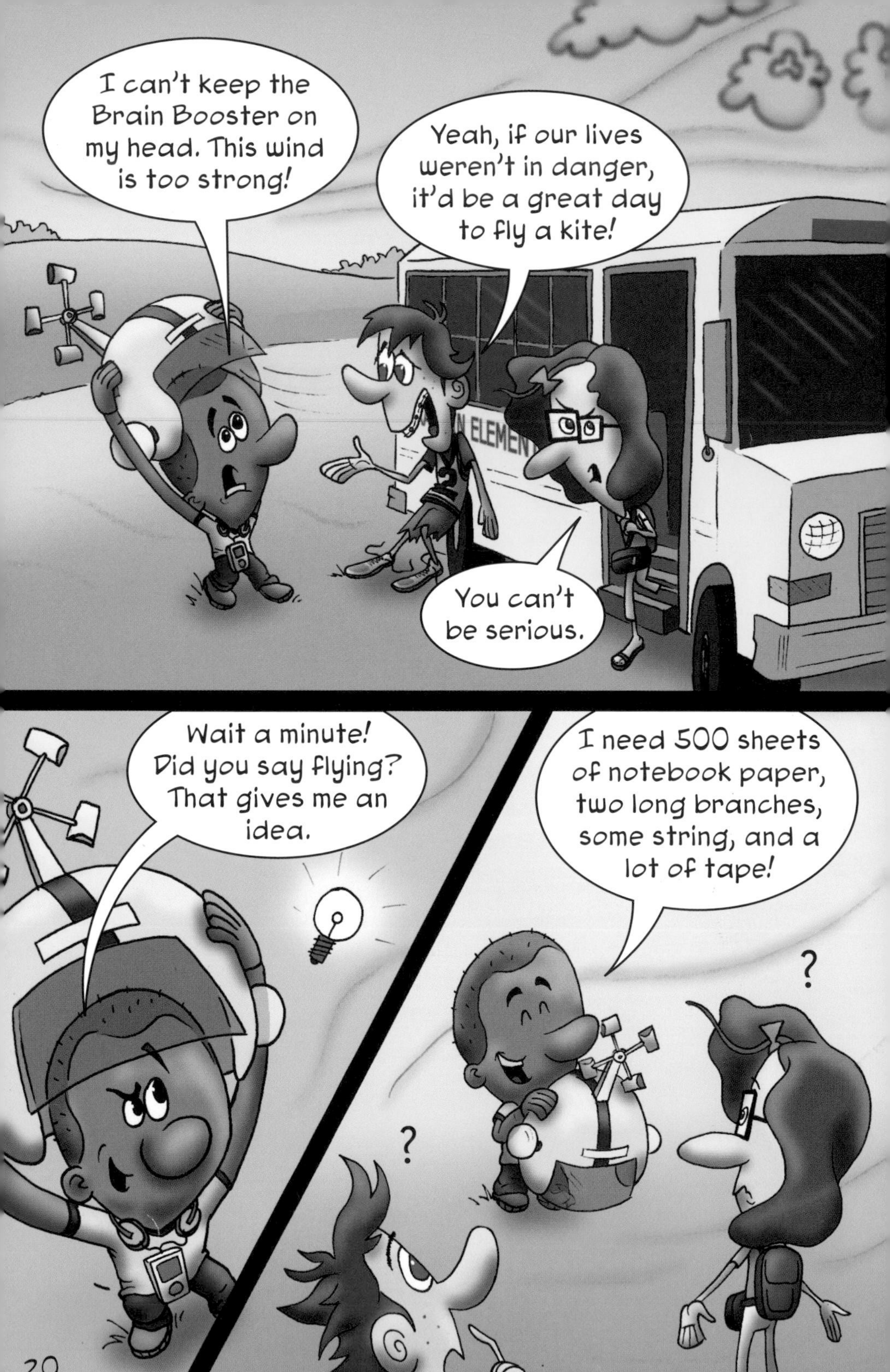
I can't keep the Brain Booster on my head. This wind is too strong!
Yeah, if our lives weren't in danger, it'd be a great day to fly a kite!
You can't be serious.
Wait a minute! Did you say flying? That gives me an idea.
I need 500 sheets of notebook paper, two long branches, some string, and a lot of tape!
?
?

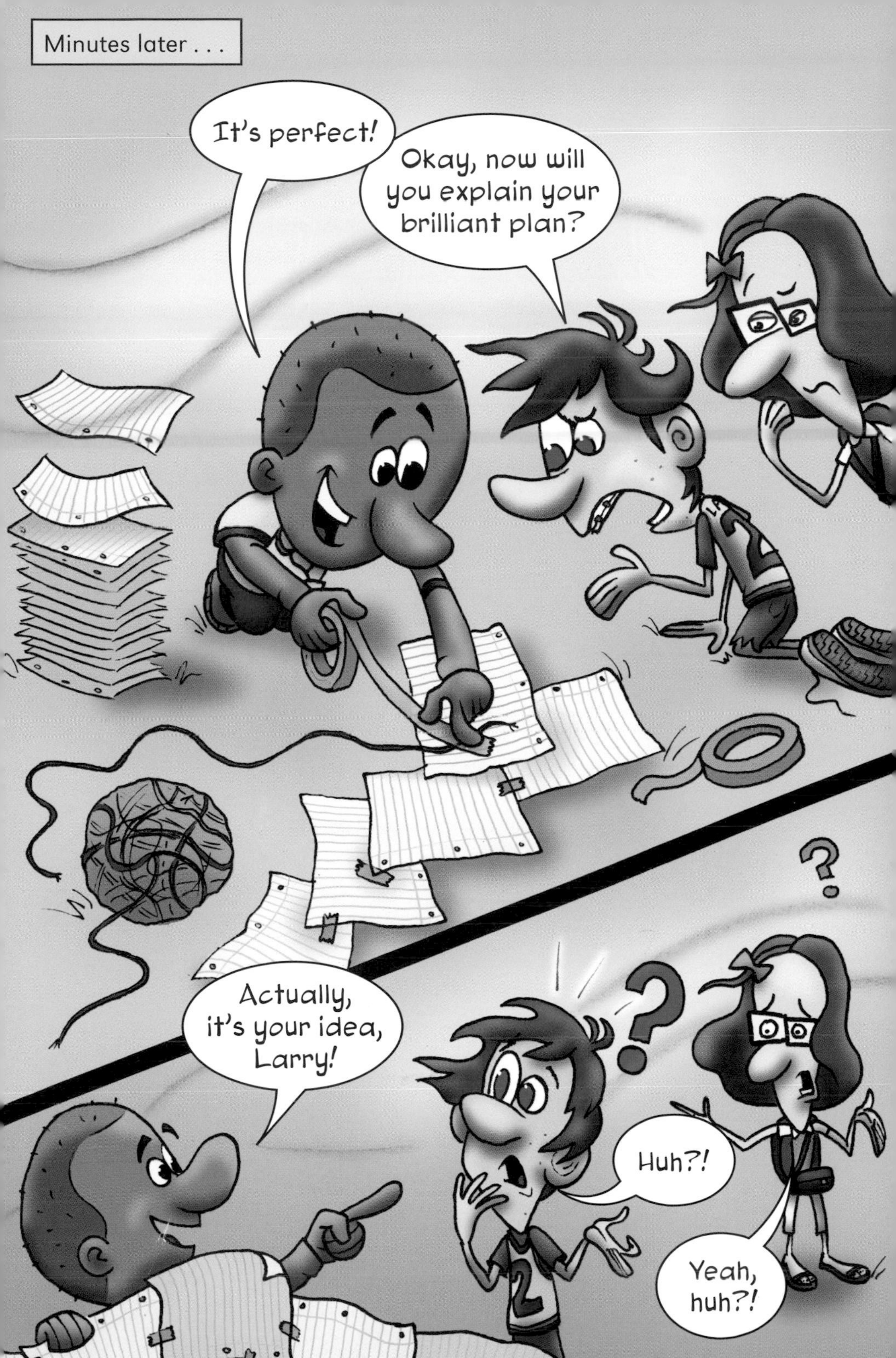
Minutes later . . .
It's perfect!
Okay, now will you explain your brilliant plan?
Actually, it's your idea, Larry!
Huh?!
Yeah, huh?!

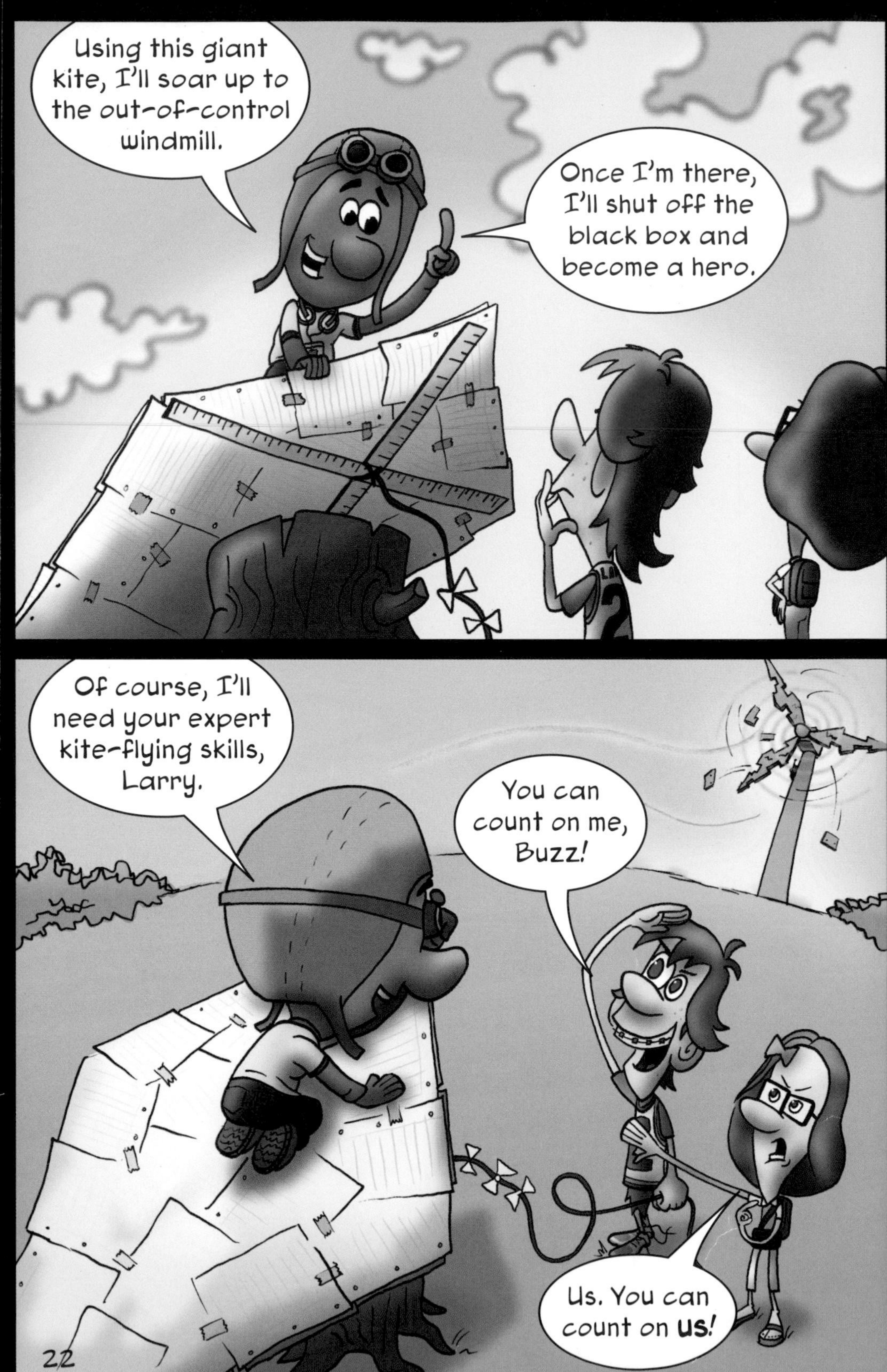
Using this giant kite, I'll soar up to the out-of-control windmill.
Once I'm there, I'll shut off the black box and become a hero.
Of course, I'll need your expert kite-flying skills, Larry.
You can count on me, Buzz!
Us. You can count on **us**!

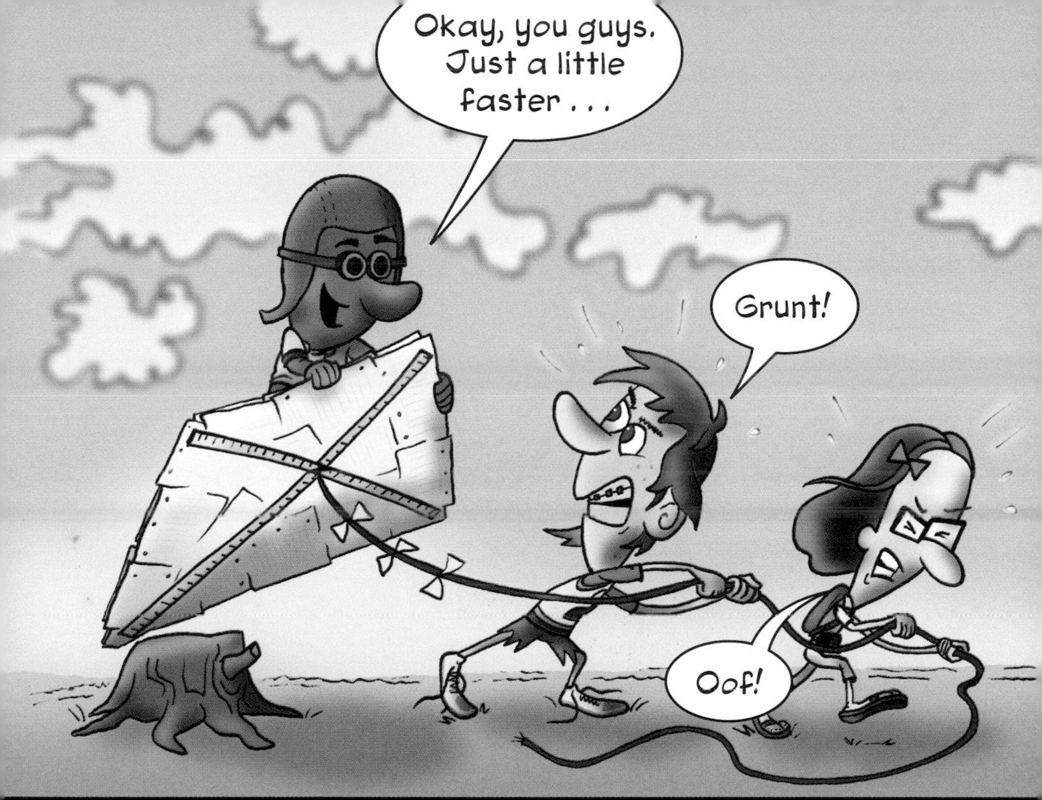
Okay, you guys. Just a little faster . . .
Grunt!
Oof!

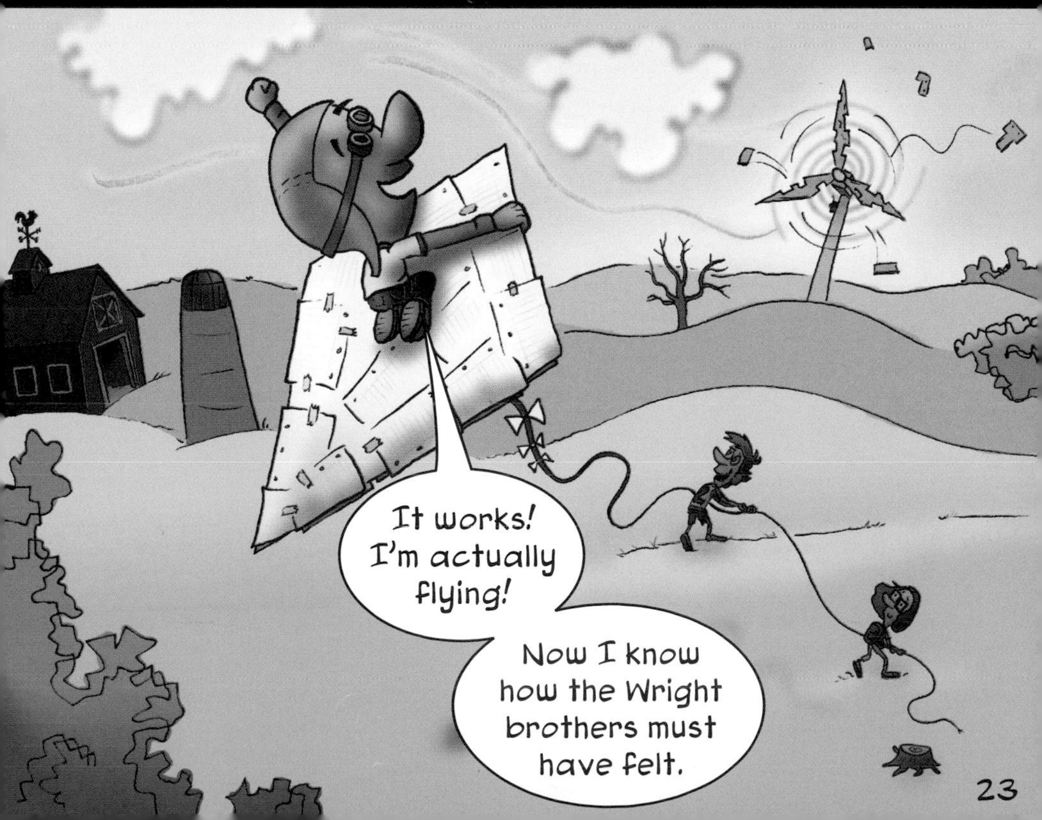
It works! I'm actually flying!
Now I know how the Wright brothers must have felt.

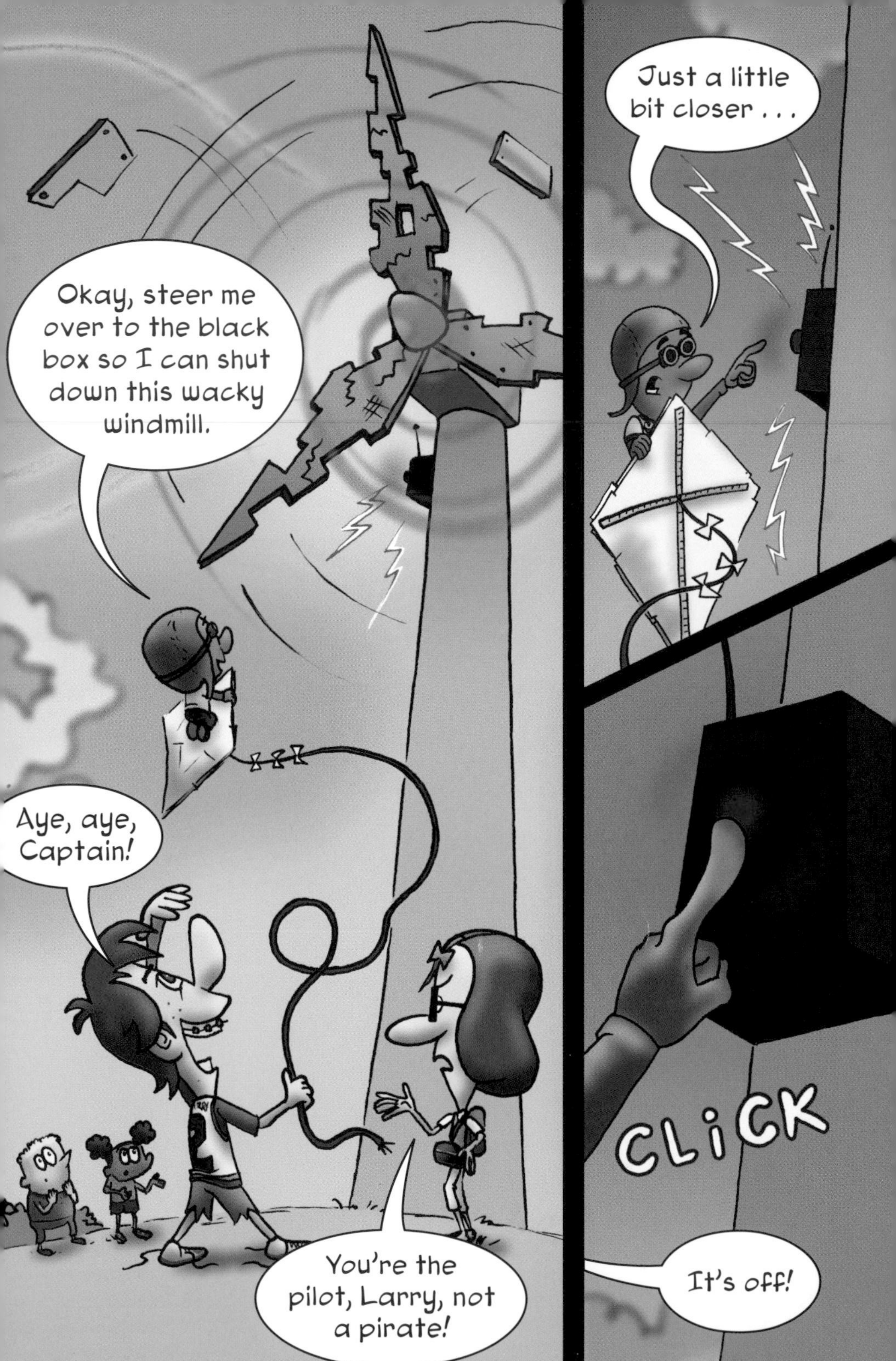
Okay, steer me over to the black box so I can shut down this wacky windmill.
Aye, aye, Captain!
You're the pilot, Larry, not a pirate!
Just a little bit closer . . .
CLiCK
It's off!

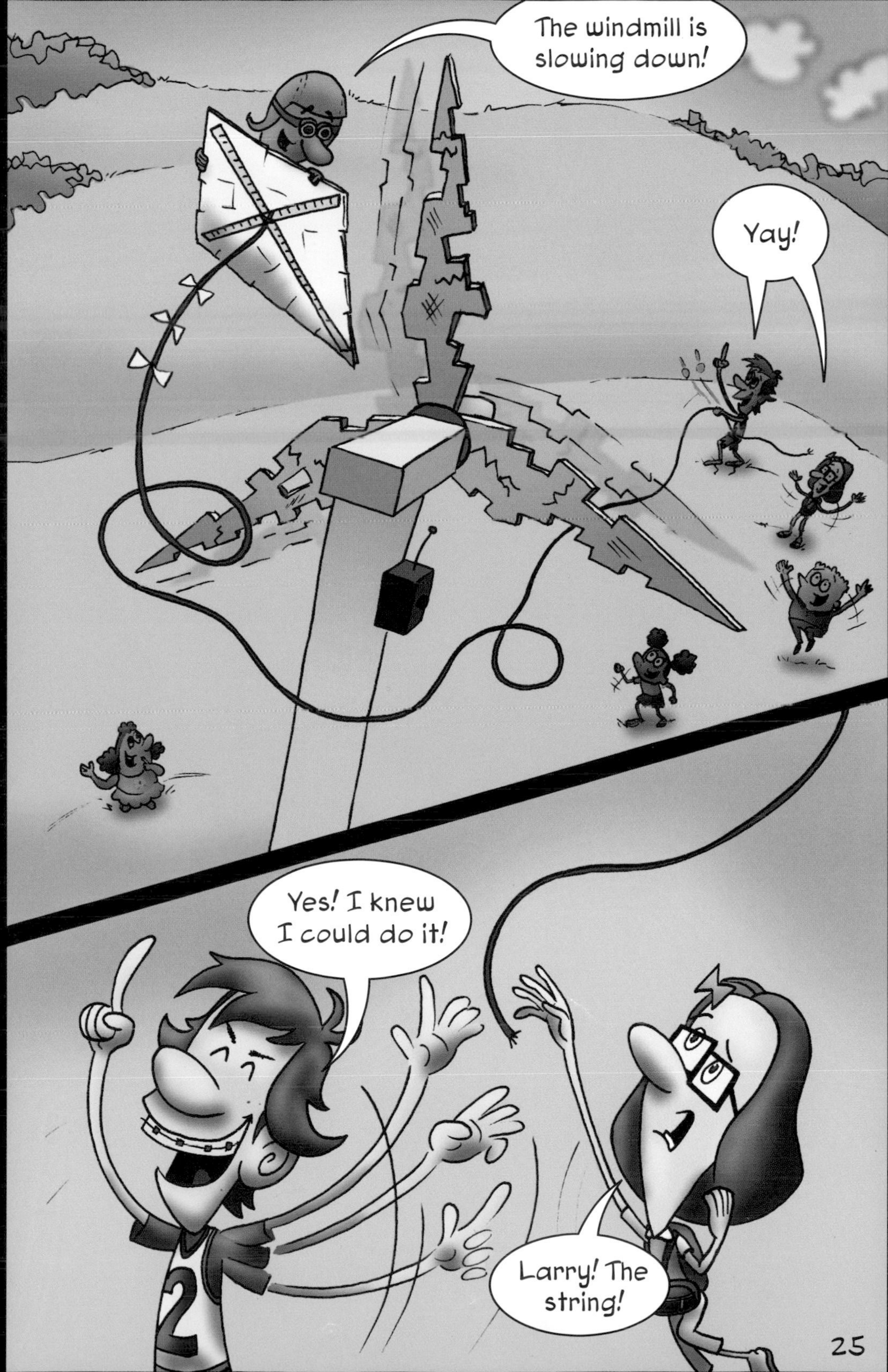
The windmill is slowing down!
Yay!
Yes! I knew I could do it!
Larry! The string!

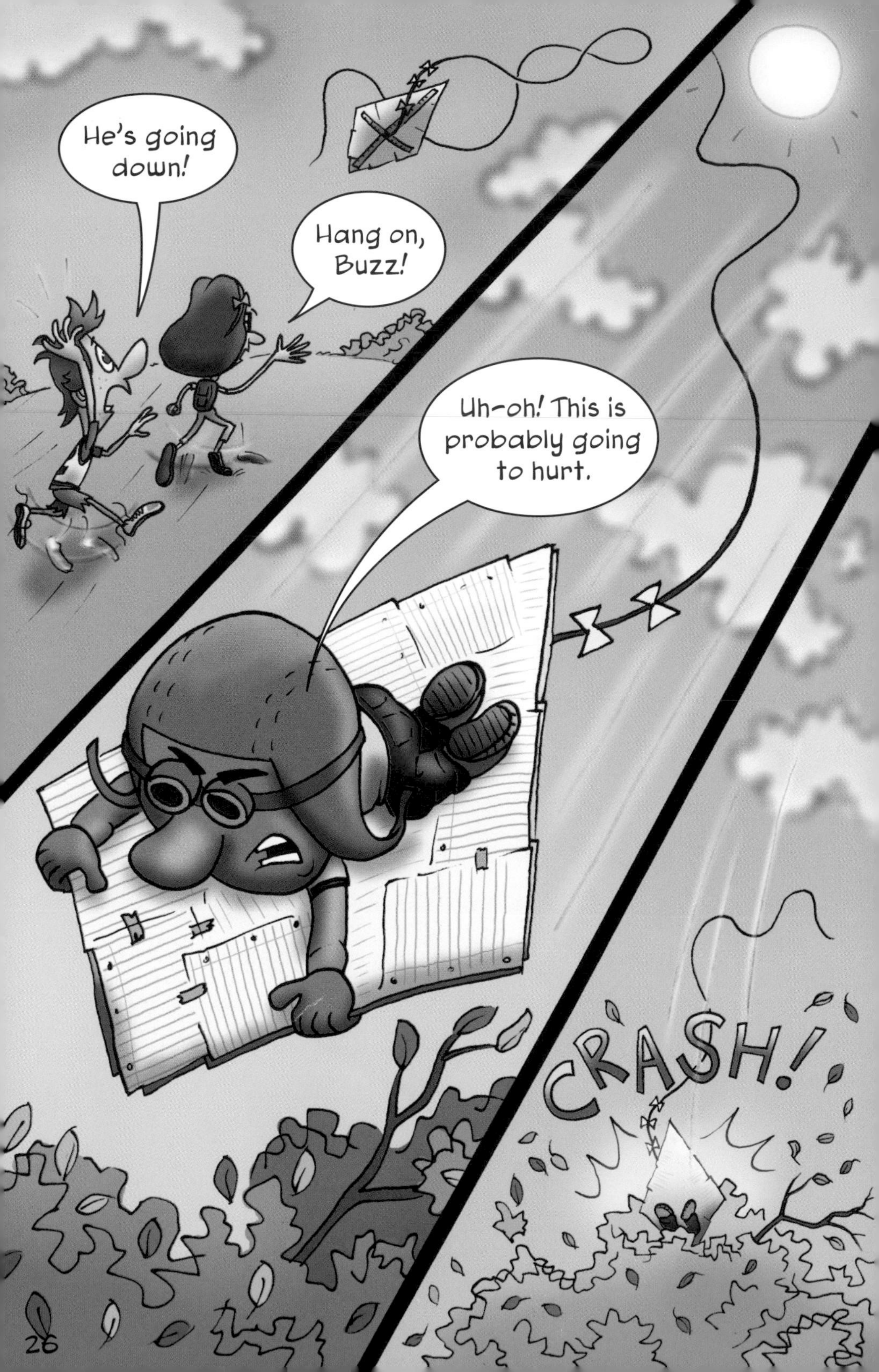
He's going down!
Hang on, Buzz!
Uh-oh! This is probably going to hurt.
CRASH!

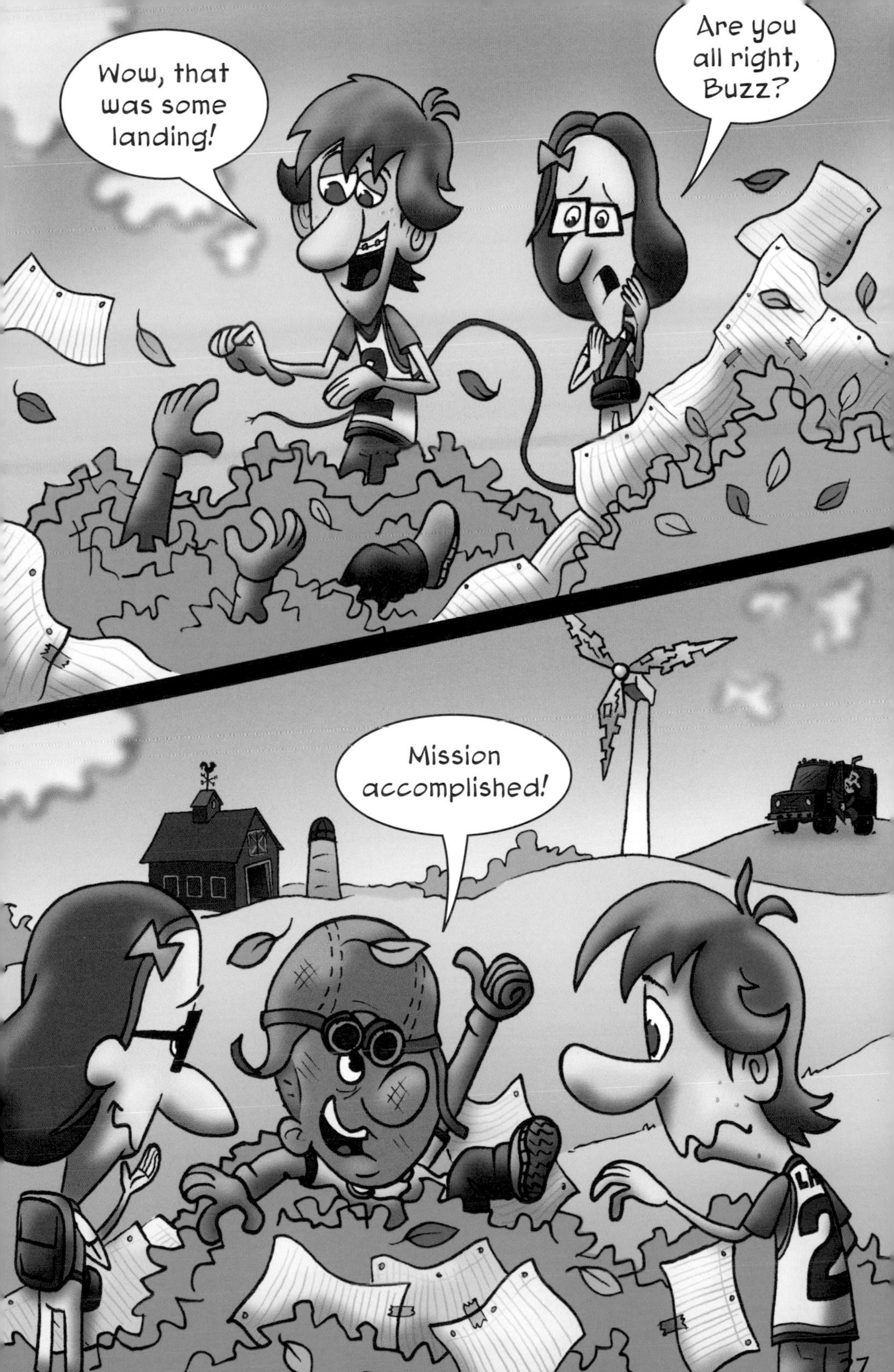
Wow, that was some landing!
Are you all right, Buzz?
Mission accomplished!

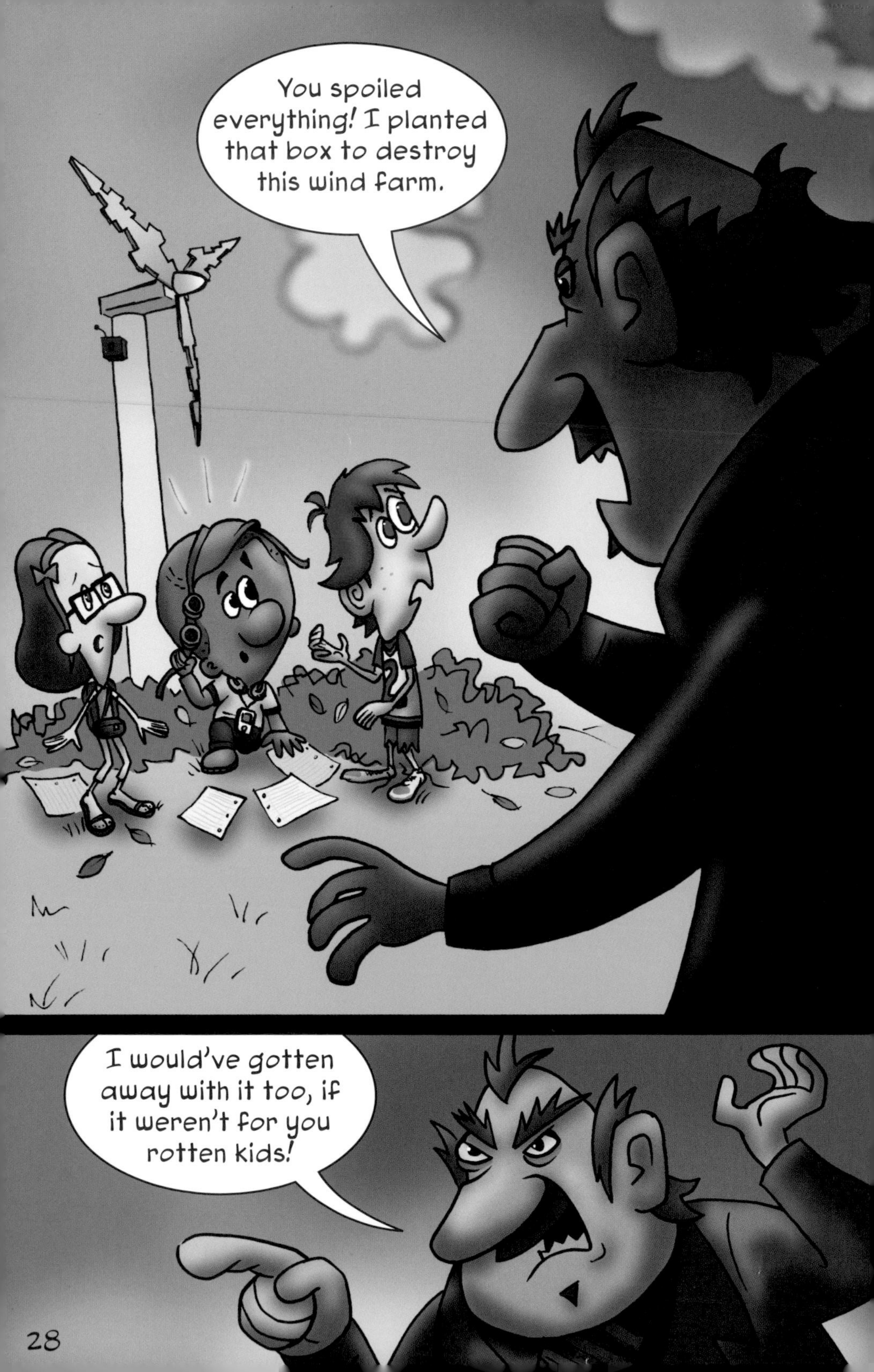
You spoiled everything! I planted that box to destroy this wind farm.
I would've gotten away with it too, if it weren't for you rotten kids!

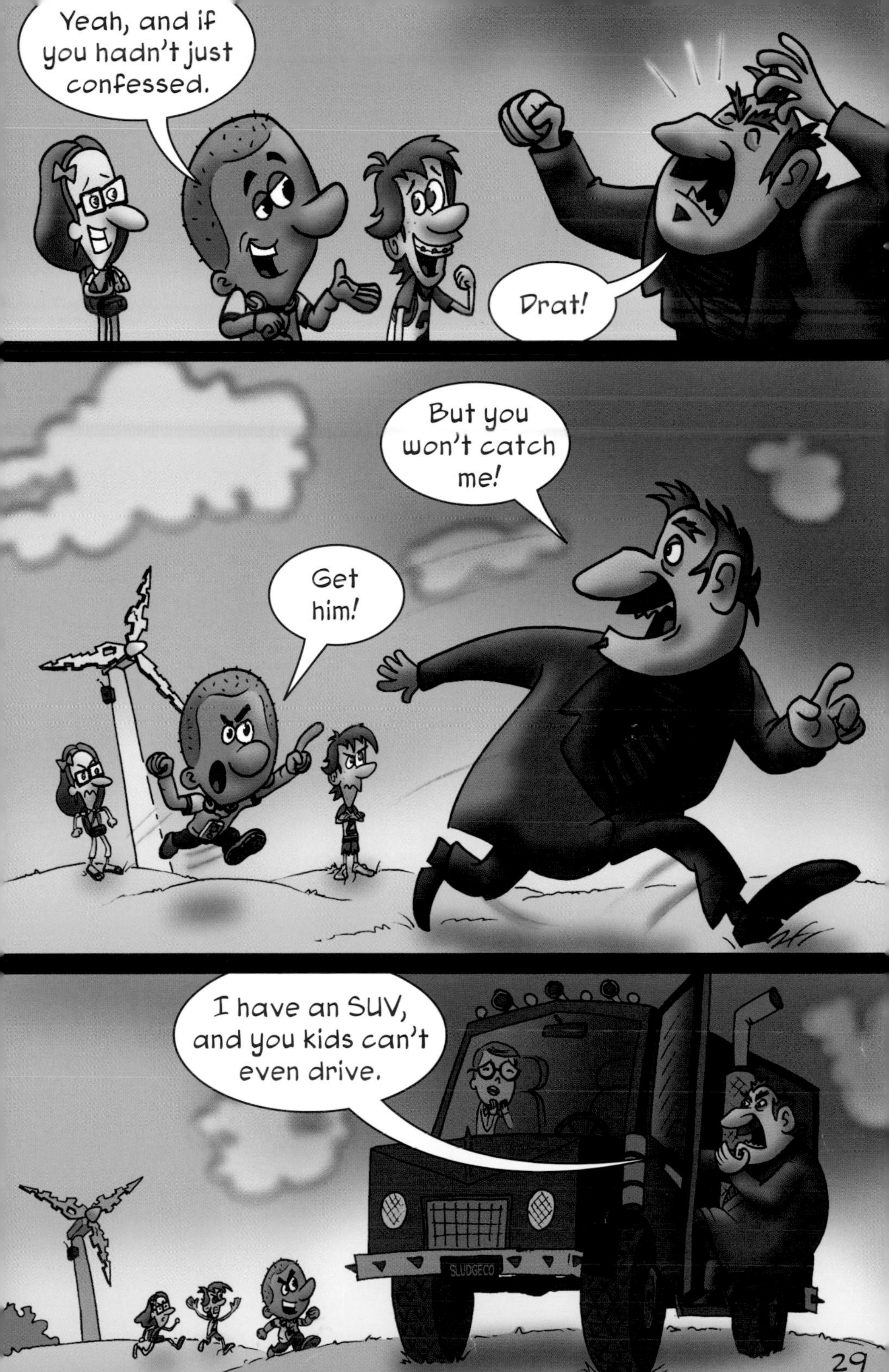
Yeah, and if you hadn't just confessed.
Drat!
But you won't catch me!
Get him!
I have an SUV, and you kids can't even drive.
SLUDGECO

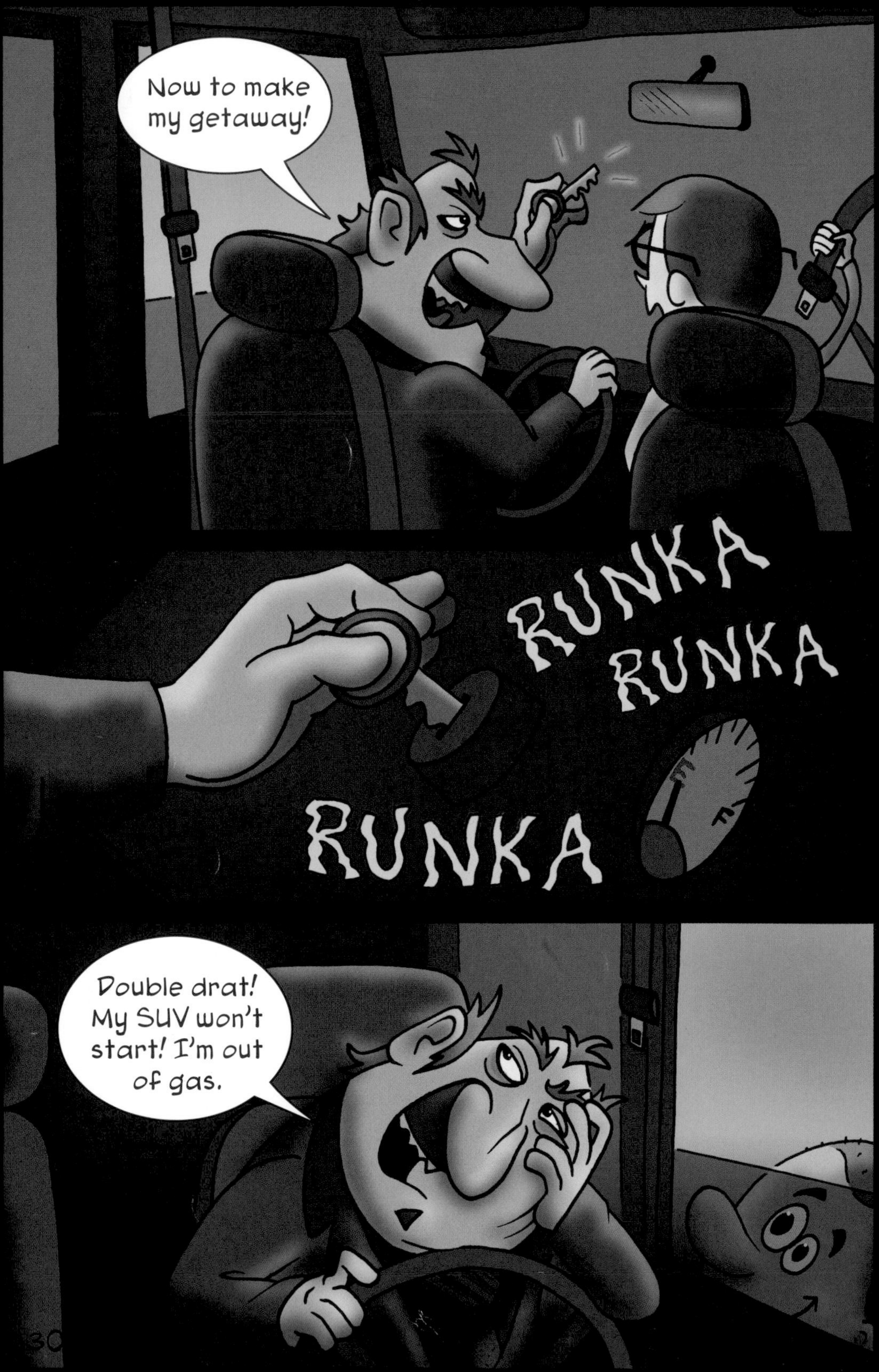
Now to make my getaway!
RUNKA RUNKA RUNKA
Double drat! My SUV won't start! I'm out of gas.

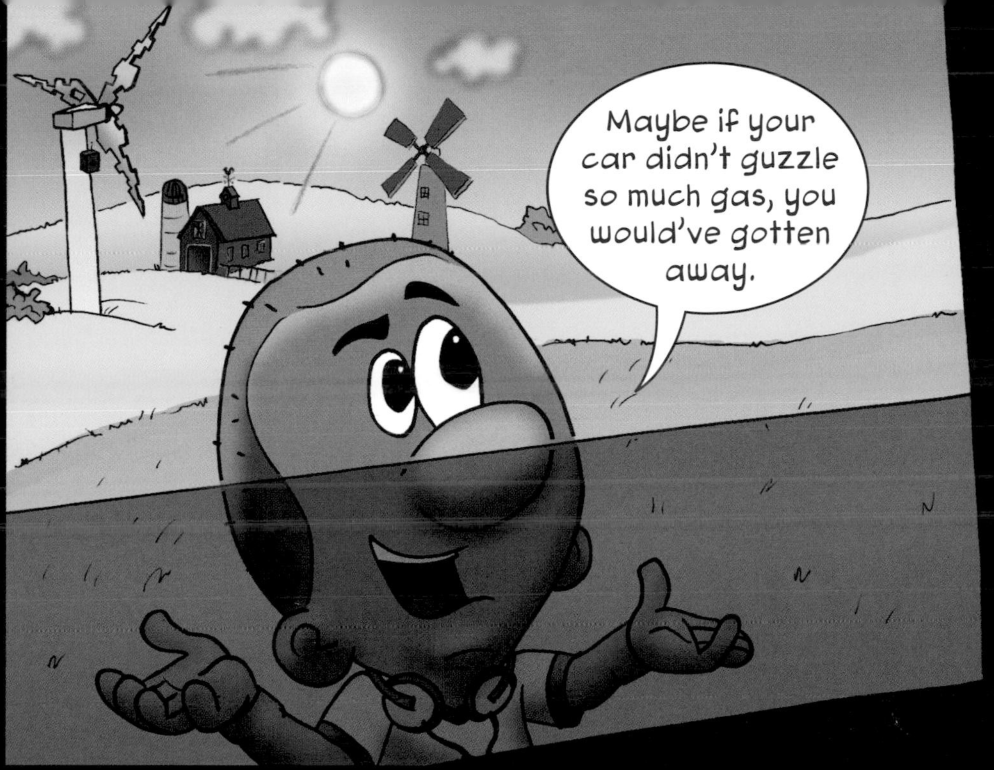
Maybe if your car didn't guzzle so much gas, you would've gotten away.

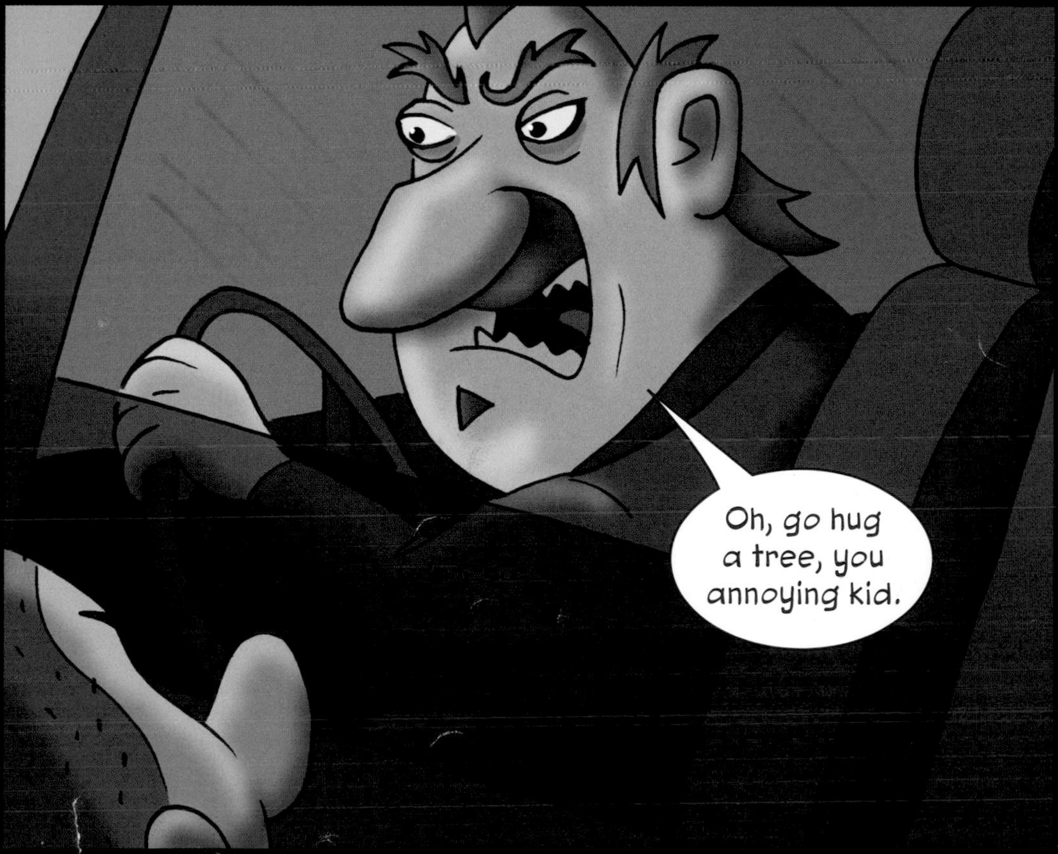
Oh, go hug a tree, you annoying kid.

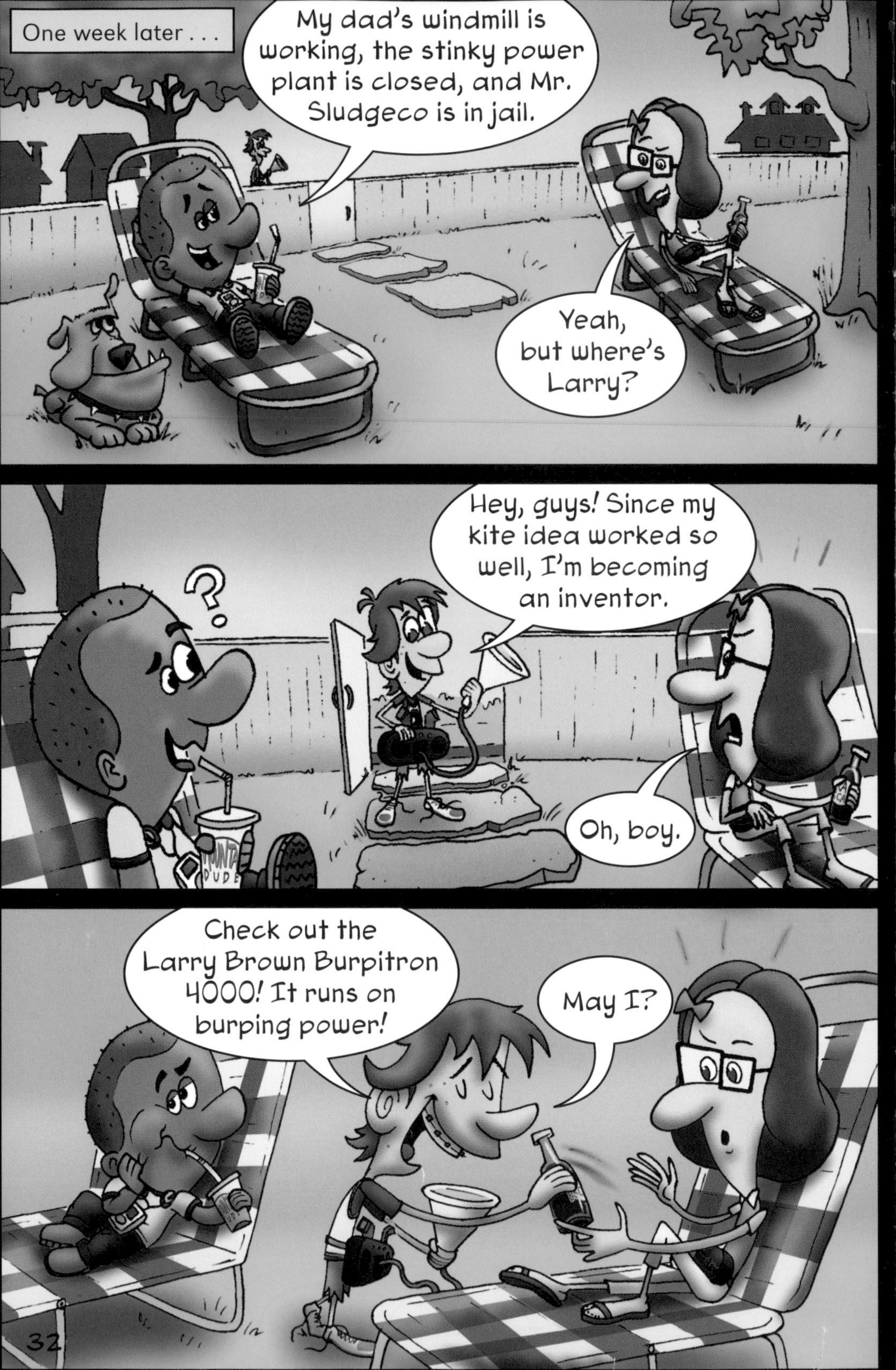
One week later . . .
My dad's windmill is working, the stinky power plant is closed, and Mr. Sludgeco is in jail.
Yeah, but where's Larry?
Hey, guys! Since my kite idea worked so well, I'm becoming an inventor.
Oh, boy.
Check out the Larry Brown Burpitron 4000! It runs on burping power!
May I?

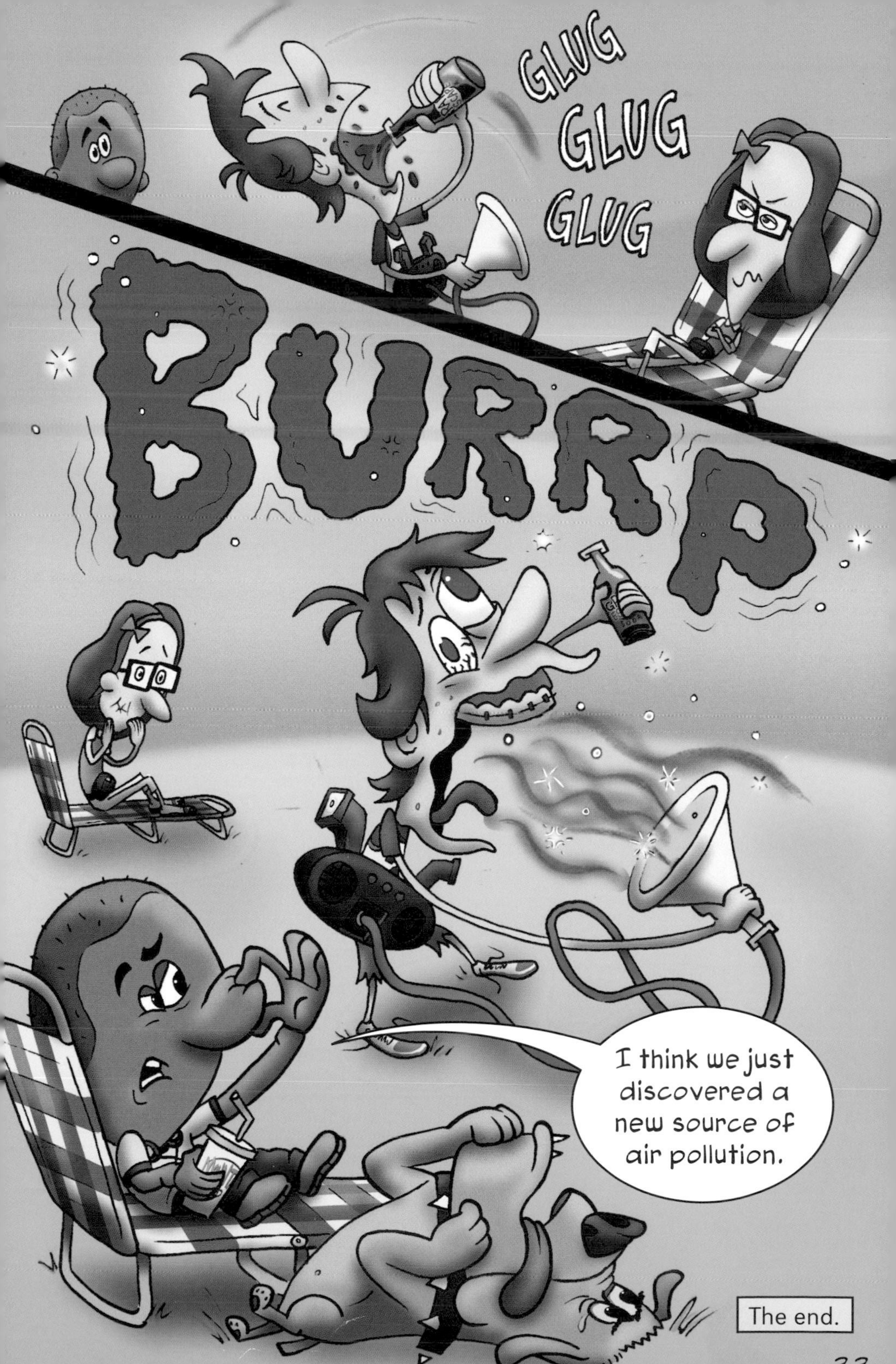
GLUG
GLUG
GLUG
BURRP
I think we just discovered a new source of air pollution.
The end.

ABOUT THE AUTHOR

Born in 1962 in Denver, Colorado, Scott Nickel works by day at Paws, Inc., Jim Davis's famous Garfield studio, and he freelances by night. Burning the midnight oil, Scott has created hundreds of humorous greeting cards and written several children's books, short fiction for *Boys' Life* magazine, comic strips, and lots of really funny knock-knock jokes. He was raised in southern California, but in 1995 Scott moved to Indiana, where he currently lives with his wife, two sons, six cats, and several sea monkeys.

ABOUT THE ILLUSTRATOR

Andy Smith knew he wanted to be an illustrator (if he couldn't be a space adventurer, superhero, or ghost hunter). After graduating from college in 1998, he began working at a handful of New York City animation studios on shows like *Courage the Cowardly Dog* and *Sheep in the Big City*. Since then, he has worked as a character designer, freelance illustrator, and taught high school and college art classes. Andy lives in Ipswich, Massachusetts, with his wife Karen.

GLOSSARY

confess (kuhn-FESS)—admit to doing something wrong

embarrassing (em-BARE-uh-sing)—something that makes a person feel uncomfortable

environment (en-VYE-ruhn-muhnt)—the natural world of the land, sea, and air

pollution (puh-LOO-shuhn)—harmful materials, such as chemicals or waste, that can damage air, water, or soil

sprain (SPRAYN)—to twist, tear, or injure a muscle, usually while exercising

supersonic (soo-pur-SON-ik)—something faster than the speed of sound

tree hugger (TREE HUH-gur)—a name sometimes given to people who want to save the environment

wind farm (WIND FARM)—an area of land with a large group of wind power machines that provide electricity

Wright brothers (RITE BRUHTH-urz)—brothers Orville and Wilbur Wright, who piloted the first powered, heavier-than-air machine

WIND POWER WISDOM

Wind energy isn't a new invention. In fact, ancient Egyptians used wind to power sailing ships more than 5,000 years ago. Early farmers in Europe and America used windmills to grind grain from their fall harvests. Today, wind machines called turbines turn wind energy into electricity that can power our homes and schools.

In 1888, inventor Charles F. Brush (1849–1929) built the first windmill used to create energy.

The amount of electricity a turbine creates depends on its size. Located in Germany, the world's largest wind turbine is a whopping 453 feet (138 meters) tall! This giant machine creates enough power for 5,000 homes.

Wind farms, also known as wind power plants, are groups of turbines used to create electricity. Some wind farms have only a few turbines. The largest wind farm, located in Taylor County, Texas, has 421 wind turbines.

Large wind machines need winds of 13 miles per hour (6 meters per second) to create electricity. They are often located where winds are the most powerful, such as shorelines or open plains. Today, some wind machines are even built on platforms in the ocean.

More than half of the states in America use wind energy to create electricity. Texas, California, Iowa, Minnesota, and Oklahoma are the top wind energy states in the country.

In 2008, scientists believe wind energy will power more than 4.5 million homes in the United States. Although this may seem like a lot, it's only about 1% of the total electricity the country will use.

With nearly 19,000 wind machines, Germany has more turbines than any country in the world. About 5% of the country's total electricity comes from wind power.

DISCUSSION QUESTIONS

1. Buzz Beaker's dad invented a windmill to stop pollution and help save the environment. What are some things you can do to help the environment?

2. Each page of a graphic novel has several illustrations called panels. What is your favorite panel in this book? Describe what you like about the illustration and why it's your favorite.

3. Describe some of the ways Larry and Sarah helped their friend Buzz Beaker in this story. Do you think Buzz could have stopped Sludgeco's evil plans without them? Why or why not?

WRITING PROMPTS

1. Buzz's field trip to the wind farm turned out to be pretty exciting. Describe the most exciting field trip you've ever been on. Where did you go? What made the trip so much fun?

2. In this story, Buzz's dad and Larry each created a wacky invention. Write down your own idea for an invention. What does it do? How will it help people? Give your invention a name and draw a picture of it.

3. In this story, we learn that Buzz's friend Sarah is extremely smart. But we don't learn much else about her. Write your own story about Sarah's family, friends, pets, and hobbies.

INTERNET SITES

The book may be over, but the adventure is just beginning.

Do you want to read more about the subjects or ideas in this book? Want to play cool games or watch videos about the authors who write these books? Then go to FactHound. At *www.facthound.com*, you'll be able to do all that, and more. The FactHound website can also send you to other safe Internet sites.

Check it out!